The Slickers

SELECTED FICTION WORKS BY
L. RON HUBBARD

FANTASY
The Case of the Friendly Corpse

Death's Deputy

Fear

The Ghoul

The Indigestible Triton

Slaves of Sleep & The Masters of Sleep

Typewriter in the Sky

The Ultimate Adventure

SCIENCE FICTION
Battlefield Earth

The Conquest of Space

The End Is Not Yet

Final Blackout

The Kilkenny Cats

The Kingslayer

The Mission Earth Dekalogy*

Ole Doc Methuselah

To the Stars

ADVENTURE
The Hell Job series

WESTERN
Buckskin Brigades

Empty Saddles

Guns of Mark Jardine

Hot Lead Payoff

A full list of L. Ron Hubbard's
novellas and short stories is provided at the back.

*Dekalogy—a group of ten volumes

The Slickers

Published by
Galaxy Press, LLC
7051 Hollywood Boulevard, Suite 200
Hollywood, CA 90028

Printed in the United States of America.

ISBN-10 1-59212-357-0
ISBN-13 978-1-59212-357-5

Library of Congress Control Number: 2007903615

Contents

FOREWORD · vii

THE SLICKERS · 1

MURDER AFLOAT · 31

KILLER APE · 75

STORY PREVIEW:
THE CHEE-CHALKER · 103

GLOSSARY · 113

L. RON HUBBARD
IN THE GOLDEN AGE
OF PULP FICTION · 121

THE STORIES FROM THE
GOLDEN AGE · 133

Stories from Pulp Fiction's Golden Age

AND it *was* a golden age. The 1930s and 1940s were a vibrant, seminal time for a gigantic audience of eager readers, probably the largest per capita audience of readers in American history. The magazine racks were chock-full of publications with ragged trims, garish cover art, cheap brown pulp paper, low cover prices—and the most excitement you could hold in your hands.

"Pulp" magazines, named for their rough-cut, pulpwood paper, were a vehicle for more amazing tales than Scheherazade could have told in a million and one nights. Set apart from higher-class "slick" magazines, printed on fancy glossy paper with quality artwork and superior production values, the pulps were for the "rest of us," adventure story after adventure story for people who liked to *read*. Pulp fiction authors were no-holds-barred entertainers—real storytellers. They were more interested in a thrilling plot twist, a horrific villain or a white-knuckle adventure than they were in lavish prose or convoluted metaphors.

The sheer volume of tales released during this wondrous golden age remains unmatched in any other period of literary history—hundreds of thousands of published stories in over nine hundred different magazines. Some titles lasted only an issue or two; many magazines succumbed to paper shortages during World War II, while others endured for decades yet. Pulp fiction remains as a treasure trove of stories you can read, stories you can love, stories you can remember. The stories were driven by plot and character, with grand heroes, terrible villains, beautiful damsels (often in distress), diabolical plots, amazing places, breathless romances. The readers wanted to be taken beyond the mundane, to live adventures far removed from their ordinary lives—and the pulps rarely failed to deliver.

In that regard, pulp fiction stands in the tradition of all memorable literature. For as history has shown, good stories are much more than fancy prose. William Shakespeare, Charles Dickens, Jules Verne, Alexandre Dumas—many of the greatest literary figures wrote their fiction for the readers, not simply literary colleagues and academic admirers. And writers for pulp magazines were no exception. These publications reached an audience that dwarfed the circulations of today's short story magazines. Issues of the pulps were scooped up and read by over thirty million avid readers each month.

Because pulp fiction writers were often paid no more than a cent a word, they had to become prolific or starve. They also had to write aggressively. As Richard Kyle, publisher and editor of *Argosy*, the first and most long-lived of the pulps, so pointedly explained: "The pulp magazine writers, the best of them, worked for markets that did not write for critics or attempt to satisfy timid advertisers. Not having to answer to anyone other than their readers, they wrote about human beings on the edges of the unknown, in those new lands the future would explore. They wrote for what we would become, not for what we had already been."

Some of the more lasting names that graced the pulps include H. P. Lovecraft, Edgar Rice Burroughs, Robert E. Howard, Max Brand, Louis L'Amour, Elmore Leonard, Dashiell Hammett, Raymond Chandler, Erle Stanley Gardner, John D. MacDonald, Ray Bradbury, Isaac Asimov, Robert Heinlein—and, of course, L. Ron Hubbard.

In a word, he was among the most prolific and popular writers of the era. He was also the most enduring—hence this series—and certainly among the most legendary. It all began only months after he first tried his hand at fiction, with L. Ron Hubbard tales appearing in *Thrilling Adventures, Argosy, Five-Novels Monthly, Detective Fiction Weekly, Top-Notch, Texas Ranger, War Birds, Western Stories,* even *Romantic Range.* He could write on any subject, in any genre, from jungle explorers to deep-sea divers, from G-men and gangsters, cowboys and flying aces to mountain climbers, hard-boiled detectives and spies. But he really began to shine when he turned his talent to science fiction and fantasy of which he authored nearly fifty novels or novelettes to forever change the shape of those genres.

Following in the tradition of such famed authors as Herman Melville, Mark Twain, Jack London and Ernest Hemingway, Ron Hubbard actually lived adventures that his own characters would have admired—as an ethnologist among primitive tribes, as prospector and engineer in hostile climes, as a captain of vessels on four oceans. He even wrote a series of articles for *Argosy,* called "Hell Job," in which he lived and told of the most dangerous professions a man could put his hand to.

Finally, and just for good measure, he was also an accomplished photographer, artist, filmmaker, musician and educator. But he was first and foremost a *writer,* and that's the L. Ron Hubbard we come to know through the pages of this volume.

This library of Stories from the Golden Age presents the best of L. Ron Hubbard's fiction from the heyday of storytelling, the Golden Age of the pulp magazines. In these eighty volumes, readers are treated to a full banquet of 153 stories, a kaleidoscope of tales representing every imaginable genre: science fiction, fantasy, western, mystery, thriller, horror, even romance—action of all kinds and in all places.

Because the pulps themselves were printed on such inexpensive paper with high acid content, issues were not meant to endure. As the years go by, the original issues of every pulp from *Argosy* through *Zeppelin Stories* continue crumbling into brittle, brown dust. This library preserves the L. Ron Hubbard tales from that era, presented with a distinctive look that brings back the nostalgic flavor of those times.

L. Ron Hubbard's Stories from the Golden Age has something for every taste, every reader. These tales will return you to a time when fiction was good clean entertainment and the most fun a kid could have on a rainy afternoon or the best thing an adult could enjoy after a long day at work. Pick up a volume, and remember what reading is supposed to be all about. Remember curling up with a *great story.*

—Kevin J. Anderson

KEVIN J. ANDERSON *is the author of more than ninety critically acclaimed works of speculative fiction, including* The Saga of Seven Suns, *the continuation of the* Dune Chronicles *with Brian Herbert, and his* New York Times *bestselling novelization of L. Ron Hubbard's* Ai! Pedrito!

The Slickers

The Slickers

TEX LARIMEE inserted his cigar below his scraggly mustaches and looked sideways at the stranger.

"Yep," said Tex, "I'm on my way to New York, and I'm here to tell you right now that if any of these greenhorns tries to pull anything on Tex Larimee, they'll have to talk it over with Judge Colt first."

He patted the bulge under his coat and, in doing so, displayed his bright sheriff's badge to momentary view.

The stranger tilted his bowler hat and suppressed a smile with his hand. The stranger had a diamond on his finger which matched the glitter of his hard eyes.

Tex, supposing that this partner in the smoking car had come there by chance, talked on.

"Old John Temple knows where to go for help," said Tex, nodding his head vigorously and gnawing harder on the mangled cigar. "He wouldn't trust none of those city dicks. He sent right out to Arizony for his old friend Tex Larimee."

"Who's John Temple?" said the stranger.

"What," said Tex, "you ain't never heard of John Temple? Why, snap my suspenders, but you Easterners are the most ignorant . . .Well, he's the biggest copper man in Arizony, that's what. He's got more millions than you got whiskers.

He's so rich he uses solid gold cuspidors, that's what. An' you never heard of him."

"Huh-uh," lied the stranger, fingering the diamond. "What'd he send for you for?"

"Why, to guard him, o'course. Out in Arizony, a man don't need no guardin'. Why, you could leave a million dollars sittin' in the middle of the street and nobody would think of packin' it off. But New York—wal, that's different. They'd slit your throat for a nickel in that town, I hear. John Temple, he ain't in such very good health and he wanted me to come East and bring him back home. And here I am."

"You're sheriff out there or something, aren't you?" said the stranger.

"Sure . . . Say, how'd you know?"

"Oh, you just look like a sheriff, that's all. I could spot your kind most anyplace. Big black hat, gray mustaches, high-heeled boots . . . Sure, I know your kind when I see one."

"Sheriff of Cactus County," said Tex, proudly. "Been sheriff for thirty years and they don't show no signs of kickin' me out yet."

The stranger got up and elaborately stretched. "We're passing Newark," he said. "I think I'll go get my baggage together. See you later, Sheriff."

"S'long," said Tex, looking out of the window.

The stranger went up the aisle, opened a door and passed into the next car. He promptly collared a porter and thrust a five-dollar bill into his hand. "Here, take this telegram and send it when we stop at Newark, understand?"

Tex was uncomfortable sitting on the red plush. He squirmed and shifted his gun into an easier position. He looked at the maze of chimneys which went sailing past and shook his head.

"Beats hell," said Tex. "Ain't even room to breathe out this way. No wonder John Temple wants to go home."

A few minutes later, after the stop at Newark, the train screeched to a stop in Pennsylvania Station. Tex picked up his paper suitcase and followed the other passengers down to the platform. Suspiciously, he thrust away the redcaps.

"Beats hell," said Tex. "These here Easterners ain't even strong enough to carry their own suitcases."

Disgustedly he stalked up the iron steps to the waiting room, intending to phone John Temple at the Manhattan Hotel.

The crowd was thick and noisy. Tex Larimee, standing a head taller than most of the men, gouged his way through the press, eyes yearningly fixed on the red-and-gold sign far away which said "Phones."

"Beats hell," said Tex. "Regular damned stampede."

A sallow-faced man was coming the other way. His face was thinner than a knife blade and his eyes were hot. He ran squarely into Tex. The press of the crowd held him there for a moment.

Tex shoved him away but the man was hurled back at him again.

"Doggone," said Tex, "you can't walk through me. What do you think I am? A shadow?"

The sallow-faced one drifted out and away and Tex lost

sight of him. Presently the crowd thinned and Tex made his way toward the phone signs.

He leaned over the switchboard desk. "Please, ma'am, would you call up the Manhattan Hotel for me?"

The girl glanced up, startled by the mustaches and the big black hat. "Five cents, please."

Confidently, Tex reached into his pocket. He scowled and tried another. He set down the suitcase and rapidly searched through his coat.

A baffled expression came over his leathery face. "Beats hell. I put that wallet right there in my hip pocket and I . . ."

"Five cents, please," said the girl in a mechanical voice.

Tex repeated the search and then it began to dawn upon him that he had been robbed. Hastily he felt for his gun. It was gone. He grabbed for his star and clutched nothing but vest cloth.

The girl frowned and held her earphones on tight. A policeman came up and motioned with his stick. "Move along, buddy."

"Look here," said Tex, looking earnestly at the beefy red face before him, "I'm Sheriff Tex Larimee of Cactus County, Arizony. I—"

"That so?" said the cop. "Move along, buddy, before I have to get tough with you."

"Tough with me?" said Tex, backing off to give himself arm room. "Look here, you shorthorn, when you bark at me—"

"Move along," said the cop.

A thin finger tapped the sheriff's shoulder. Full of fight, Tex whirled and found himself facing the stranger he had met on the smoking car.

"Having trouble?" asked the man in the bowler hat.

"I been robbed," cried Tex. "I was coming through that crowd and some sticky-fingered coyote went through me like a bullet through butter. And then this blankety-blank beef steer—"

"What's that?" said the officer, juggling his nightstick.

"You heard it!" roared Tex.

Nervously, the stranger tugged at the sheriff's arm. "You better come along with me, mister. It won't do you any good to buck the law."

Tex picked up the paper suitcase and, still growling, followed his newfound friend out of the station and into the din of Seventh Avenue.

"We better have a drink," said the stranger, tipping the bowler hat forward on his milk-white brow.

Tex yelled, "All right, but I've got to call the Manhattan Hotel."

"Call from the bar," said the stranger.

Overawed by the hurry and bustle and noise, feeling small in this dingy canyon of buildings, Tex tagged along, high-heel boots scuffing the pavement, spur rowels whizzing.

They entered a small barroom on Thirty-fourth Street, where the stranger seemed to be known.

"Better go into the back room," said the stranger. "More quiet back there."

Tex was still too worried about his money and papers to protest and he stepped through the door. The place was dimly lighted and poorly furnished with scarred tables and unpainted chairs.

A sleek-headed waiter took their order and slipped out with it.

"What the hell's the matter with people in this town?" said Tex. "They stare at you like you was something out of a museum." He gave his big black hat a defiant tug and then straightened his mustache. "I don't think I like this place. All my life I wanted to see New York and now I'm here, to hell with it."

"Oh, you have to get used to it," said the stranger.

"I don't think I'd live long enough," said Tex, "what with all them taxis scootin' around. Them drivers act like they was breakin' broncs. Where's the phone around here?"

Tex started to get up. A chilly voice behind him said, "Don't move, Bronson, and that goes for you, too, old-timer."

Tex turned carefully around. He knew that tone of voice. A man had slipped into the door and stood with his back to it holding a .45 automatic carelessly pointed in the general direction of the table. The fellow wore a checkered suit and a flaming red tie. His nose had been broken back against his face and his mouth was an ink mark across his off-side jaw.

Bronson froze where he was and his eyes grew very round.

"I told you never to come back to this town, Bronson. I told you and I thought you'd have better sense. Get up careful and walk into that other door, understand?"

Bronson got up. Tex showed no inclination of moving at all. Tex's eyes were roving up and down the checkered suit.

Bronson whispered hoarsely, "Do what he says. He's a killer."

Tex turned disgustedly and followed Bronson into the indicated room. The place was without lights or furniture. They stumbled over some mops and pails and the door slammed shut behind them. The key rasped in the lock.

Tex upended a pail and sat down on it. "Damn it, I've got to call the Manhattan Hotel. Will that gent be gone long?"

"Not long enough," sighed Bronson.

"What's he goin' to do?"

"Get his pals and a car."

"What for?"

Bronson sighed again. "Looks like we're going for a ride."

"Will we be gone long?"

"You don't understand," said Bronson. "We'll be gone a long, long time. They're going to take us out and bump us off."

"You mean they're goin' to plug us? What the hell? I never did nothin' to them. And if they want to kill us, what'd that gent walk off for, huh? Why didn't he just plug us and get it over with?"

"He has to get his mob," said Bronson.

"That's a helluva way to go about it," said Tex. "I don't like this town more and more and besides, John Temple'll be gettin' worried about me."

They sat there in the dark for a long time. Tex chewed up

half a bar of tobacco, using a mop pail for a spittoon. Bronson burned a pile of cigarettes.

Finally Tex stood up. "I ain't going to wait."

"No, no," said the stranger, quickly. "You—"

Tex drowned out the rest of the sentence. Tex raised his heel and banged it against the lock. He tried it again, kicking harder.

With a crash the door flew open. Tex stalked out into the second room and tried that door. It was also locked. Tex raised his boot and slammed it against the door. With a shower of splinters it caved in.

Tex strode out into the barroom. Several men were sitting around with surprised looks on their faces, but the gunman was not in sight.

Tex walked out on the sidewalk and proceeded toward Sixth Avenue, glaring at every man who stared at him.

He found a cop on the corner and received directions about the Manhattan Hotel. It was up in the Fifties, a long, long walk from Thirty-fourth.

In spite of his high heels, Tex walked it and his indignation against his reception committee grew with every stride.

"Had to get his gang," muttered Tex. "Had to get his gang. The yellow-bellied sidewinder. The pasty-faced son. Had to get his gang and there he stood with his gun in his hand and neither of us . . . Hell!"

At last he found the Manhattan Hotel. He had never seen a hotel with phone service in the rooms before so he walked straight past the switchboard.

Finally Tex stood up. "I ain't going to wait."

He asked the clerk, "Where can I find John Temple, sonny?"

The smooth-faced clerk eyed Tex with distrust. "You have some business with—"

"Never mind about my business," snarled Tex. "If you slick-ears ain't the nosiest pack of lobos I ever see . . . What room's he got? Quick now."

He got the room number immediately and bore down upon the elevators. He had ridden in elevators before, but he had never trusted them any. He stepped gingerly into a car and was whisked to the twentieth floor, leaving his stomach in the region of the tenth.

Getting out, he prowled the halls until he found the number he wanted. He began to beam. John Temple was near at hand and all his troubles would be over.

He knocked and then knocked again without receiving any answer. He tried the door and found it open.

At first glance the room appeared empty, and then he saw a curiously stiff hand jutting out from the other side of the bed.

Tex stalked across the rug and then came up with a jolt.

John Temple was lying with outflung arms in a muddy pool of his own blood. A knife wound showed in his throat, another in his chest. His jaw was frozen open. His gray hair was matted.

Tex stood there for at least two minutes without moving a muscle. He turned slowly around and saw that the room had been ransacked.

"Something," muttered Tex, "has got to be done."

He marched toward the door he had closed behind him, but before he could touch the knob it swung in to him.

Two men in plain clothes were standing in the hall. Behind them was an officer in uniform.

"Okay, Haggarty," said one of the detectives. "Look around the room."

The other, Haggarty, stepped inside and spotted the corpse.

"Dead man," said Haggarty in a matter-of-fact voice.

"Okay," said his partner, walking up to Tex. "Don't get excited, grandad." With deft fingers he frisked Tex for a rod and found only the empty holster.

"Knife job, shivved him twice," said Haggarty.

"No knife," said the other.

"Must have pitched it out," said Haggarty.

"Stand right there, grandad," said the other, "and maybe if you act nice, you'll get treated better. O'Brien, put the cuffs on him."

The uniformed officer snapped the bracelets on Tex's weathered wrists and gave him a hard look.

Haggarty said, "Call the gang and get them down here, Smitty."

Detective Smith tossed the phone from cradle to his hand and asked for police headquarters.

"Gimme the squad," said Smith.

"Hello, that you, Pat? Send up the dead wagon for a stiff at the Manhattan Hotel. . . . Sure, it's murder just like the tip said. Sure, we got the guy. Think we sleep all the time? Yeah, he's right here. Looks like revenge or something. . . . I dunno, funny old geezer in a big hat. . . . How do I know what the stiff's name is? Come up and find out yourself."

Tex came to life. "Say, what the hell are you fellers tryin' to do, huh? This ain't right. Look here, you think I done that? You think I'd use a knife? Why, by the great horned spoon, old Temple was my best friend. What's the matter with you fellers? Say, listen, don't you know who I am? I'm Tex Larimee, sheriff of Cactus County, Arizony, that's who. Look here, I got—"

"Shut yer trap," said O'Brien. "You'll talk. Later."

"Damn it, look here," said Tex, suddenly worried, "Temple sent for me to come to New York and see him home. . . ."

"Yeah, we believe you," said Haggarty, searching the room.

"Now, see here," said Tex. "I've got a telegram from him."

"Let's see it," said Smith.

Tex, in spite of the bracelets, tried to get into his breast pocket. With a sinking feeling he remembered that all his papers, even his suitcase, were gone.

"Look here," said Tex, "you just wire Ed Murphy at Stud Horse, Arizony, and he'll—"

"*Will* you shut up?" said Haggarty.

Something like a wolf howl came from the street and presently the room was full of cops and fingerprint men and medical examiners.

Worried though he was, Tex looked at this young army of police officers and grinned sourly to himself. "Hell, back in Arizony there's just me. And I never make a mistake like that. Damned if—"

"Shut up," said O'Brien.

A police lieutenant stopped before Tex and looked him over. "Haul him down to headquarters and he'll talk all right. He'll talk."

"Come along," said O'Brien, jerking Tex's arm.

The officers pried their way through the crowd in the lobby and to the Black Maria. Tex felt red about the ears. People were pointing at him.

The wagon careened through the traffic, first on one pair of wheels, then the other.

"What's the idea of drivin' so fast?" said Tex. "I ain't anxious to get anyplace."

The police driver cut three red lights in a row, played hopscotch with a streetcar, squeezed in between two trucks at forty miles an hour, siren and whistle going continually.

With squawking brakes they lurched up against the curb before headquarters. Tex was hurried up the steps, through the doors, down a hall, into an elevator, out of it, into an office, into another office and then into a room which had an enormous green-shaded lamp in the middle of it.

They slammed him down into a chair, snapped off the cuffs, turned the light straight into his eyes and began to yell at him.

Tex was so confused he could not do more than blink. He could not hear any one of the men. All of them were going hard.

Suddenly there was silence. A lieutenant of detectives stepped into the light and thrust his jaw into Tex's face.

"So you won't talk, hey?"

"Damned right I'll talk. Good God, you're yappin' like a lot of coyotes over a dead horse. Sure I'll talk, but maybe some of you ought to listen, huh?"

"All right, wisenheimer," snapped the lieutenant. "Then answer this: Why did you kill John Temple?"

15

"I tell you," yelled Tex, "I didn't kill him. He was a friend of—"

"Cut it," said the lieutenant. "We want it straight. Why did you kill John Temple?"

"Look here," bawled Tex, mustaches sticking straight out in his fury, "I'm Tex Larimee, sheriff of Cactus County, Arizony, that's who, and you can wire Ed—"

"Why did you kill John Temple?"

"You can wire Ed Murphy and he'll tell you who—"

"Why did you kill John Temple?"

"I came here to see old John and take him home and I—"

"Why did you kill John Temple?"

"He made a mint of money in the copper mining—"

"Why did you kill John Temple?"

"And he wanted me to look after him while he—"

"Why did you kill John Temple?"

"And I met a stranger on the train named Bronson and he—"

"Why did you kill John Temple?"

"And when I was coming up the steps a guy picked my pockets—"

"Why did you kill John Temple?"

"And he stuck us up and told us he was going to—"

"Why did you kill John Temple?"

"And when I walked into the room, there he was on the floor—"

"Why did you kill John Temple?"

"He must have had a lot of pesos on him and—"

"Why did you kill John Temple?"

"And that's all I know about it," finished Tex, defiantly.

"So you won't talk, hey?" snarled the lieutenant. "Slam him behind the bars, Fallon, and leave him there. Okay, wisenheimer, if you won't talk now, you'll talk later. We got a rubber hose around here for tough birds like you. Take him away!"

They hustled Tex down another hall, into an elevator, down it and into another hall, and suddenly Tex found himself staring at the back of a locked cell.

A sleepy-eyed man looked up from the bunk, grunted, turned over and went to sleep again.

"Beats hell," said Tex. "More and more I don't like this here town."

Tex sat down and rested his chin on his palms.

About nine the next morning, the lieutenant sent for Tex Larimee and soon Tex was ushered into that august presence.

"Now look here, wise guy, we ain't got all day. You come clean and we'll get this out of the way." He eyed Tex up and down. "From the West, ain't you? Well, you ain't West now. Maybe out there you can go around stabbing guys, but this is New York, understand? And in New York, we've got LAW."

"I'm the law out there," said Tex, sullenly, gnawing at the ends of his mustache. "And from what I've seen of this here—"

"Why did you kill John Temple?" said the lieutenant, exactly like a parrot.

"You ask me that again," said Tex, "and I ain't guaranteeing what I'll do about it."

17

"Tough guy, hey?" said the lieutenant. "You know who you killed? You killed John Temple the Copper King, that's who. He's worth ten million dollars and that makes it important, get me?"

"What if he was only worth two bits?" said Tex.

"Now come clean," said the lieutenant. "Why did you kill John Temple?"

Tex merely glared. An office clerk came in, listened for a moment and then pointed at the lieutenant's desk.

Annoyed, the lieutenant glanced down at a medical examiner's report and recommendation. He studied it for some little while, evidently having difficulty reading. He moved his lips, scratched the top of his bald head and then stared up at Tex.

"Who the hell are you, anyway?" said the lieutenant.

Tex let out a long sigh. "I'm Tex Larimee, sheriff of Cactus County, Arizony. I came here to New York to take John Temple home. He wired me and I—"

"Send for Lefkowitz," said the lieutenant.

Lefkowitz came after a long delay. He was short, round-faced and businesslike. His attitude said that he didn't have all day to waste on a mere cop.

"Now what?" barked Lefkowitz. "I've got work to do. Am I the medical examiner here or the errand boy?"

"Now, Doc," said the lieutenant, placatingly, "does this report of yours read right?"

"No, I make them out for fun," snapped Lefkowitz.

"Look here," said the lieutenant, "you say this John Temple

had been dead almost three hours when we found him. That right? How'd you know how long he'd been dead?"

"Rigor mortis and body temperature told me that. . . . Say, what the hell is this? I said he'd been dead almost three hours and that's all there is to it, understand?"

"I say he couldn't have been!" yelled the lieutenant, surging out of his chair and banging his fist down on the report. "It ain't possible. This bird killed him. We walked in and there he was, going through the bureau. Whatcha got to say about that, Mister Medical Examiner? Maybe if you had my job—"

"The hell it isn't!" roared Lefkowitz, also banging his fist down on the desk. "What's the matter with this guy happening in after the cadaver was knifed, eh? What about that?"

The lieutenant paced up and down the rug. He picked up the report, threw it down, picked it up and hit it with his fist. "Damn that clerk. He said this bird went up just before we did. He said he couldn't mistake him because of that mustache and black hat. And now you come along and shoot my case all to pieces. Damn it, I've got to get a conviction if I have to hang the mayor. John Temple was worth ten million dollars. That makes it important, see? What am I going to do if every mother's son in this office comes around and shoots my cases full of holes? What do ya think you are, anyway?"

Lefkowitz turned on his heel and opened the door. "That's my report and that's all there is to it. And if you call me again when you've got my report in front of you, I'll see you *never* get a conviction."

19

The door slammed and the lieutenant looked hard at Tex. "I still think you did it."

Tex spat thoughtfully at the cuspidor and then looked at the two cops who held him as though measuring up their fighting capacities.

The lieutenant looked back at the report, baffled. Tex said, "Well, what'll it be? You goin' to hang me or what?"

"Turn him loose," said the lieutenant to the two cops. "And listen here, you. We're keeping an eye on . . . I mean we're not through with this yet. Now get out."

Tex planted his big black hat on the back of his head, turned around and walked out.

Hands thrust into his empty pockets he stared balefully at the noisy, hurrying street and the towering buildings. He sighed deeply and looked down at his feet. It was a long walk back to Thirty-fourth Street.

He was buffeted about by the crowd until he found out that the only way to walk in New York was dead ahead without caring who you knocked down. After that he made fair progress.

Accustomed as he was to looking thirty miles in any direction without seeing anything more startling than a Joshua tree, Tex had some difficulty finding the bar. He walked around and around the blocks adjacent to Pennsylvania Station, high heels hurting worse and worse. By the time he had run out of epithets for pavement and people he noticed that he kept seeing one particular man always behind him.

The fellow was round and beefy and red-faced and he walked with a heavy list as though about to fall over. Once Tex walked straight back to where the fellow stood and then, for fear he was mistaken, allowed him to go on peering into the shop window.

After all, thought Tex, you couldn't tell these damned greenhorns apart, nohow.

Again he searched for the bar, and he found plenty of bars but none of them looked just right. Once more he noticed the fat one behind him.

It dawned upon Tex then that headquarters was shadowing him, hoping that he'd lead them to some of his supposed pals. Tex thought that over.

It takes a long time for an Arizonian to get mad. He has lots of time and lots of space to get mad in and he usually ends up without getting mad at all. But this was different. People were bumping him; an El was grinding overhead; a block away, the Seventh Avenue subway was yowling under his skittish feet and three thousand cabs were honking their horns.

Tex walked straight back to the shadow and grabbed him by the coat. The man was so startled the cigarette jumped out of his mouth and showered sparks down his vest.

"What the hell's the idea?" roared Tex. "Maybe you think I can't read trail sign, huh? Maybe you think I need a conducted tour around this here town. Wal, I don't."

He gave the detective a thorough shake and then dropped him to the pavement.

"If," said Tex in a mounting bellow, "if I see you once more I'm going to lick the whole damned police force. You better get going."

The shadow scuttled back. This was unprecedented. He could hardly call for aid because to do that would be to admit that he had shadowed so poorly that he had been detected in the act. He made the best of it by half walking, half running out of sight.

Tex whirled around and strode up the block again. This time he was successful. Without pausing in his stride he stomped into the barroom and up to the bar.

The bartender recognized him and went a little ashy. Tex's face was as grim as an Indian's.

"WHERE'S BRONSON?" said Tex.

"I . . . I dunno. I ain't been—"

"Where's Bronson?" roared Tex, snatching hold of the man's white coat.

"He . . . he ain't here," gasped the bartender, badly shaken.

Tex, oblivious of the men in the room, strode toward the rear door which he knew would lead to his late prison. He had seen other doors branching off that one.

Entering the dingy room, he saw a door open on the far side. With three quick, catlike steps he went up to it, pressed it gently back as though air had blown it that way, and peered in.

A man with a face as narrow as a knife blade was sitting on the edge of an iron cot. His hot eyes were thoughtful as he stared at the smoke which coiled up from his marijuana cigarette. His white shirt was crisp and the cuffs and collar were unbuttoned.

It was the man who had collided with Tex in the station.

Tex stepped in and stood there, hands in his pockets, looking pensively at his victim.

The man started up. Tex gently pushed him back to a sitting posture. The man's eyes darted hopelessly toward his jacket which hung from a nail.

"Where is it, sonny?" said Tex.

"Where's what?" whined the victim.

"My old pal Judge Colt. Come on, sonny."

There was a certain quality in Tex's gaze which pinned the young man down as though he had an Apache arrow through him. Tex walked sideways toward a rough bureau. The pickpocket tried to rise excitedly. Tex calmly sat him down again.

With quick fingers, Tex rifled the bureau. The first thing which came to light was his six-gun. He balanced it fondly, spun it a couple times and then cocked it with a horny thumb. He dished up his wallet and a packet of papers and pocketed them. In the corner he spotted his paper suitcase, still closed up.

"All right, sonny," said Tex. "When's he come in?"

"Who?"

"Your boss."

"In about . . . He never comes in here."

"In about an hour, you say? All right, sonny, we'll just sit down and wait a spell. You ain't restless, are you? Bad for the heart to git restless, sonny. You just sit there in sight of the door smoking that cigarette and we'll wait for Bronson."

Tex sat down behind the door. The pickpocket tried to sit still but he kept itching in various spots.

An old alarm clock on the bureau ticked away minutes very slowly. Tex seemed quite complacent. He had reached the deadly calm stage when he could hit nickels at a hundred yards with a .45. He had felt like this numerous times before, always just before a killing.

Two hours passed before Bronson showed up. He came in with a quick, nervous step, heading straight for the pickpocket's bedroom.

Bronson stopped in the door and fanned himself with his bowler hat. "We got to make tracks, Gino. They let the old fool loose and he'll—"

"Who'd they let loose?" said Tex, standing up.

Bronson's jaw sagged. His hand darted for his shoulder. A horrible click filled the room. The six-gun under the horny thumb was at full cock. Bronson stared straight down the tunnel.

"We'll go for a walk," said Tex, slowly chewing his words. "Sonny, you git on your coat and come right along. And you can carry that suitcase while you're about it."

Tex herded them toward the barroom. He heard a door hinge creak behind him.

Tex rolled sideways.

An automatic spat flame out of the shadows.

Tex sidestepped again.

The hard-faced young man in the checkered suit had come in through the back entrance. He was leaning far to the right, trying to chop down on Tex's elusive shape.

The six-gun roared.

The checked suit was rumpled. It caved forward very slowly, getting pink just over the heart. Tex heard the cloth and the gun hit the floor. He had already turned to see Bronson hauling at his own automatic.

Tex fired for the man's wrist. The gun flew out of the holster and hit the ceiling. Bronson grabbed for his arm.

Men were scurrying around out in the barroom. Tex did not know how much time he had left.

With a quick push, Tex slammed Bronson back against the wall.

"This," said Tex, "is going to be a short and sweet execution. I ain't got no time for formalities. This is coldblooded murder."

"Owwww," moaned Bronson.

The pickpocket, Gino, cowered in the corner.

"You want to talk, Bronson?" said Tex.

"Go . . . go to the devil!" Bronson shouted in his pain.

The door bulged inward and suddenly men burst into the back room. Stepping hurriedly away from them, Tex had them covered before they saw him.

It was the police lieutenant and the detectives Smith and Haggarty.

"Stand back, you jaspers," barked Tex. "This is my roundup."

"Put up that gun, you fool," yelled the lieutenant.

Haggarty foolishly tried to get at his own roscoe. Tex sent his hard hat sailing into the air with a snap shot.

The lieutenant, Smith and a police officer who had followed them in stood very still with open mouths. Haggarty was somewhat foolishly feeling for his bowler.

Tex backed further away and turned to Bronson. "I said this was going to be coldblooded murder. And that's what it'll be, cops or no cops. Make your peace, Bronson."

With a slow downthrow, Tex began to pull the trigger. The six-gun leaped back and up. A button flew from Bronson's coat.

Everybody in the room let out a breath.

Tex clucked his tongue and muttered, "Can't seem to hit nothin' anymore."

"Do something!" wailed Bronson.

Tex swept down again with his gun. Bronson was twisted half away from him. The roar of exploding powder blasted the room. Bronson's necktie fell in half at the knot.

"Damn it," muttered Tex, "I'm gittin' old."

He raised the gun a third time and brought it slowly down. Bronson was paralyzed. His jaw was hanging open as if he had a billiard ball between his teeth. His eyes were glassy.

Tex fired.

A button flew from Bronson's sleeve.

"I'll talk!" screamed Bronson. "Quit it! I'll talk. Listen," he begged, "that guy murdered Temple." He pointed at the faintly stirring mound of checked suiting.

"How do you know?" said Tex, casually sighting the gun again.

"Don't! Don't shoot. I know because I told him to."

"I don't believe you," said Tex, bringing the gun lower and lower and squeezing the trigger as he did so.

"No, wait, listen. I'm telling the truth, so help me! I been shadowing Temple. I been after him for six months. I knew he was sick and I knew he'd send for you. So I shadowed you from Arizona to New York. I waited until you were almost there and then I ordered Johnny to knife him.

"I had Gino pick your pocket in the station. I had Johnny come back and hold us up to make it look like I was still your friend. I called the cops when you went up to the hotel."

"I don't believe it," said Tex, starting to sight the gun again. He was twenty feet or more from Bronson, but, to Bronson, the gun was apparently ten inches from his chest.

"I had to kill him," wailed Bronson. "He was buying up all my copper stock. He was trying to wreck me and I had to kill him before he ruined me. Honest, that's it. And I picked up Gino and Johnny here in New York and I paid them to—"

Gino squeaked liked a rat and tried to dive out. The lieutenant caught him and floored him with a blow to the jaw.

Tex motioned toward the checked suit and Bronson. "I suppose you gents," he said to the lieutenant, "have got enough sense to look after the rest of this. Me, I've got to catch a train for Arizony."

"Not so fast," said the lieutenant. "You're going to stay here as a material witness. This ain't cleared up well enough for me yet."

"See this?" said Tex, shaking a yellow slip under the lieutenant's nose. "That's a telegram from John Temple saying that he was afraid he would be killed and wanting me to come to New York. I'm Tex Larimee, sheriff of Cactus County, Arizony." And so saying, he carefully pinned his recovered star upon his chest.

"Oh," said the lieutenant, faintly. Then, in a louder voice, "Why the hell didn't you show me that in the first place?"

"I had to get it back," said Tex in a louder voice than ever. Then, quietly, Tex reached into Bronson's pocket and extracted a roll of money. He counted off two hundred and thirty-five dollars, the amount which had been lifted from him, and then carefully put the rest back in Bronson's coat.

"I've got to catch a train," said Tex.

"Wait a minute," said the lieutenant, an admiring smile on his face. "You sure can shoot. We thought we were pretty good around here. Of course, I never would have let you get away with that unless I thought you had some exact purpose in mind."

"Of course not," said Tex. "By the way, you better go read up on guns. All of you."

"Why so?" croaked Haggarty, surveying his blasted hat.

"Because," said Tex, opening up Judge Colt and throwing out six brass cartridges, all empty, "because there's a limit to everything. This thing's been empty for the past five minutes."

So saying, he carefully adjusted his black hat, picked up his paper suitcase and spat carefully within an inch of the lieutenant's shoe.

He marched out of the door, through the barroom, heading in a beeline for Pennsylvania Station, jumping to the right and left to avoid the taxicabs.

"More and more," muttered Tex, wrestling his bag away from a thieving redcap, "more and more I think I like Arizony."

Murder Afloat

CHAPTER ONE

Ominous Summons

THIS is Captain Simmons, Clark. I've uncovered the information you want. Come up immediately." As Bob Clark, ace operative of the Narcotics Squad, US Secret Service, listened, his long fingers tightened about the cabin phone receiver. His eyes, like hard steel, bored into the bulkhead before his face. He had received his summons to death!

"Yes, sir," he clipped.

The SS *Cubana* rolled gently in the dark swell. An orchestra played in the salon, while cocktail glasses clinked at the bar. Laughing female voices floated across the decks, tauntingly.

In front of Bob Clark's porthole, a man in trim evening clothes had stopped. The flare of the match held to a cigarette illuminated a face as sharp as a blade, eyes as black as the night. Clark was not thinking of the face, but he remembered it.

Gently he replaced the receiver and got up. From his valise he took a Police Positive .38 and a handful of shells. Drawing his gray felt hat down over his right eye, he stepped out on deck and strode forward, every nerve alert.

He had been expecting this, but the manner of its coming had been strange. In spite of the gaiety aboard the *Cubana*, he knew that death stalked the trim promenades.

The summons had been abrupt, but Clark had known immediately that he stood close to the portals of death. The voice—smooth, oily—had not been that of Captain Simmons!

Only one man aboard this ship had known that Clark was a Secret Service operator on the trail of a million and a half dollars' worth of dope. That man was the captain. Tonight, late, the captain had promised to give Clark the information as to the identity of the shipper.

But now Bob Clark knew that his light polished shoes were carrying him straight into ambush. Yet he could do nothing but go.

He ascended to the bridge. Then he stopped and watched for a moment. The captain's cabin lay but a few feet down the dark passage ahead. Clark stiffened.

Somewhere in that passage, above the roar of wind and engines, he had heard the *snick* of a gun hammer being cocked. He eased into the shadow and peered ahead.

This, then, was the trap. A crude, coldblooded attempt to murder him. Clark paused an instant to wonder where Captain Simmons might be. Had anything happened to him?

From the rack above his head, Clark took down two life preservers of the jacket type. Stringing them together, he made a panel about two feet wide and five feet long. Suddenly he thrust it out into the passage.

The preservers jerked. A slug whined off steel and out to sea. The passage flared with a sudden light, but the sound of the gun was merely a cough, the muffled sound of a silencer.

Clark dropped the preservers and stepped back. The riddled

kapok stuffing made a dark mound on the planking. In an instant the would-be murderer would come up to investigate. And then . . .

Clark drew his .38 and balanced himself against the roll of the ship.

Footsteps were coming toward him, cautious, slow, like the padding of a lynx. A black form stopped over the life preservers. Clark lunged.

He jabbed the muzzle of the gun into yielding ribs. Then the revolver was slapped to one side. A fist caught Clark under the ear. He realized that he was fighting a man of tremendous strength.

Clark's antagonist was a shimmering haze before his face. He strove to encircle the other with his arms. He battered at the face with his gun barrel. He tried to shoot, but each time his finger swept down on the trigger the gun was forced aside.

The ship rolled, making footing uncertain. Clark's opponent seemed everywhere at once.

The Federal man's hands clutched at the padded shoulders of the black overcoat. Something gave way. Abruptly, Clark lurched backward, striving to keep his feet. The empty overcoat was in his hands. The passage was deserted.

"Gone!" Clark snorted in disgust, and threw the black wrap over his arm. He strode on down to the captain's cabin. Outside the door, he hesitated, intending to knock, but through the cracks he could see no light. An almost tangible, crouching silence lay within. An odor, acrid and disagreeable, was in the air. Burning flesh!

*The Federal man's hands clutched at the padded shoulders
of the black overcoat. Something gave way.*

Clark kicked in the door and fumbled for the light switch along the wall. He found it and shot it on. Captain Simmons lay on the floor, his face twisted and gray with agony. The master of the *Cubana* was dead!

Clark jabbed his glance about the room. He sidestepped until his back was no longer toward the door. Then he turned to the body.

Simmons' shoes had been removed. A pile of matches lay beside the rumpled rug, some of them still smoldering. The soles of the captain's feet were black and charred. Clark understood then how the information about his presence aboard the *Cubana* had been obtained.

"The inhuman fiend!" he gritted. "He tortured it out of poor Simmons!"

He saw then that Simmons' fingers were tightly wrapped about a pencil. Evidently he had died slowly, horribly, but had been possessed of such great strength of will that he had forced himself to try to write out a clue to the crime.

A pack of playing cards had been spilled off the desk in the struggle. Clark noted that one of the cards was lying near Simmons' hand. It was turned face up—and it was the ace of spades.

He inspected the pasteboard under the light. On its surface, so faint as to be almost indiscernible, were several scrawled letters.

"Madame Sev——" the captain had written. After that the pencil had slid off the card.

Bob Clark did not need the last of the name.

"Madame Seville!" he finished the name aloud. "That's the information he had for me!"

That name was the key to a million and a half dollars' worth of dope which was reported to be aboard the *Cubana* at the time of her sailing from Havana.

Madame Seville was a notorious woman ally of the greatest dope smuggler in the West Indies. With the ring identified, Clark expected little difficulty in rounding up its members aboard the ship.

He would go to the first officer immediately and inform him that the captain was dead. Then, with the help of others, he would ferret out each and every suspected man on the *Cubana*. The time had come finally to crush this wholesale importation of heroin and opium. The *Cubana* was taking her last load north.

He noted the time on his wristwatch. Something made him jerk his head up to the ship's clock above the captain's desk. The hour was eight, and Clark estimated that he had been in the room for a period of at least three minutes. Something was wrong about the clock. He frowned and stared at its polished metal face. Then he knew. It had not struck eight bells.

"That's funny," he muttered, as he stretched his hand up toward the brass cylinder, intending to remove the face.

But Clark's hand never reached the dial. His back was not exposed to the door. A jog in the wall prevented that. Nor could he see the entrance from where he stood. But he heard the creak of hinges and whirled. Gun in hand, he leaped toward the panel. But he was too late.

The door was slammed and locked before he could reach it!

Clark whirled to the porthole. It was closed with a metal cover. Nevertheless, he darted out his hand and shut off the light.

The *Cubana* was lunging on through the sea without a captain, and Bob Clark, ace operative of the Narcotics Squad, was a captive on the bridge.

CHAPTER TWO

Sailor's Nightmare

CAUTIOUSLY, Bob Clark removed the disk from the porthole and stared forward toward the bow. The bridge seemed deserted. He could not see the helm, for that was above him. But he could see the fo'c's'le head across the darkness of the well deck. Several men were there, indistinguishable in the gloom.

Clark rummaged about the cabin until he found a pair of field glasses on the captain's desk. Through these he studied the men in the bow.

There were five of them, all well dressed, three of them in evening clothes. They were not talking, just staring ahead into the black night, turning occasionally to glance aft, an unmistakable attitude of waiting about them. One of them Clark saw in profile. It was the same face he had seen outside his port during the call from the bridge!

But why were these passengers on the fo'c's'le head? Were they afraid something might happen to the ship?

One of the men, chunky and fat, Clark knew. He was Harrington, head of a sugar central in Cuba. Another Clark thought he identified as Morecliff, manager of an oil company.

Perplexed, the Federal man put down the glasses and gave his attention to the problem of escape. All bells and buttons in the room had been disconnected.

Then a faint hissing sound reached his ears. As Clark listened, the sound increased.

He tried another porthole. But it was too small to permit him to pass through it. Twice he tried shouting through the porthole, but there was no response. The silence was getting on his nerves.

Even the sounds of the ship were faint. Only the plugging of the engines and the moan of the wind through the sparse rigging came to him.

Then a scent reached him. It was acrid, biting. He went to the door and sniffed vigorously. Smoke! The *Cubana* was on fire at sea!

A thin blue coil of smoke eddied through the top of the doorway. No alarm gongs were going. No feet pounded in panic across the decks. There were no sounds of boat falls. And yet the thin column of smoke curled and thickened the air in the cabin.

"What's the matter with them—all asleep?" Clark demanded of the empty cabin.

The trickery of the wind wafted a chord of music to the bridge. The orchestra was still playing. They were still dancing in the salon. Clark hammered on the pane again. Still there was no answer.

The *Cubana* had begun to yaw. The seas which had been breaking against her bows were now taking her from the port side. That meant that no hand guided the helm.

The smoke was becoming thicker, but as Clark made his way around the walls for the hundredth time, he found one corner where it was not quite so bad. He searched until he found a grating against the ceiling. This was a ventilator, leading up to the boat deck—a two-foot tube through which a man might conceivably crawl. But between Clark and freedom was the grating—built of solid steel bars.

His lungs burning with pain, Clark staggered back to the port. Thrusting his head out, he drew in a breath of smoke-tainted air.

Fumbling through the haze, Clark found the captain's desk. He drew open the drawers one by one, ran his fingers through the contents, anxiously searching for a screwdriver.

Perhaps the grating over the ventilator was removable. His fingers encountered a nail file. Clutching it tightly, he lunged for the grating.

Up on a chair, Clark found screw heads in the metal frame. He shoved the end of the file into the crevices and twisted frantically. The metal slipped.

Summoning all his willpower, Clark forced himself to relax. Panic would close this exit forever, and that would mean death. The crackle of flames was becoming louder.

Calmly now, he inserted the file into the screw head. He twisted with even pressure. His heart leaped when he felt the screw start to turn. Looking over his shoulder, Clark saw a tongue of fire jab through the charred door. Up here against the ceiling the heat was terrific.

With the first screw removed, he started on the second. There were four. He gritted his teeth against the impulse to hurry.

The second screw came away. The third screw followed. Clark dragged the grating toward him and ripped the fourth bodily from its mooring.

Pulling himself up, Clark drew his shoulders through the opening. It was a tight squeeze. He drew back again while he removed his coat and thrust it into his belt. Then he remembered the overcoat he had stripped from his assailant.

He felt for it in the dark, found it and pulled out several papers which were in the pockets.

Again he leaped up on the chair and squeezed into the opening. The ventilator was hot. It was agony each time his knees touched the metal. The air was like the blast of a furnace.

Ahead through the blackness, he saw a glimmer of light. Doggedly he crept on, until he was able to pull himself out into the chill night air.

Now he had to spread the alarm. He burst into the wing of the bridge—and stopped. The fourth officer lay in a widening pool of blood, his young face cut and beaten out of shape. Across the wheel, held upright by the swinging spokes, was the helmsman. His feet dragged the hempen mat as he moved. A steady, relentless seep of blood dripped from his skull and stained the binnacle face.

Eighteen thousand tons of steel and wood fashioned into a greyhound of the ocean were plunging unguided through the night with tongues of flame licking through the passageways.

Bob Clark slipped into his coat and swung down a ladder to a lower deck. Somewhere he would have to find an officer. Then he would hunt for the man who had done this.

Somewhere in this flaming hull lay a million and a half

dollars' worth of dope. There was a connection between it and this fire, Clark felt sure. Yet why should anyone want to destroy his own cargo?

Clark jogged into a long passage. A steward was ahead of him. The Federal man reached out and grabbed at the white jacket.

"Listen," he said. "The entire bridge is in flames. The captain is dead. Get the chief officer—tell him to get to work. There's no time to lose."

"I beg pardon, sir, but have you been drinking?" the steward asked doubtfully.

Clark smashed him flat against the steel bulkhead.

"Follow my orders!" he snapped. Something glittered in his hand—a small gold disk, the badge of the Secret Service. "Quick. We're burning at sea, understand?"

At that moment three men approached. The first was the man with the sharp face and midnight eyes. The second was fat, chunky Harrington, the sugar man. The third was Morecliff, head of an oil company.

"Anything wrong?" murmured the sharp-faced one, at the sight of Clark.

"Nothing," replied Clark as he shot a warning glance at the steward.

The man with the sharp face smiled.

"See here, fellow. My name is George Davis. I'm a stockholder in the West Indies Lines, which owns this ship. I rate the same as the captain here. If anything is actually amiss, I want to know it."

"Nothing is wrong, gentlemen," Clark answered

disarmingly. "I was just down in the fire room; the chief engineer was showing us the ship and—well—I wanted to show off in front of a young lady and I had a bit of an accident."

As Clark turned and went forward, he saw over his shoulder that the steward was walking swiftly down the passage toward the salon.

A companionway was at hand and Clark swung up toward the boat deck. The radio shack was far aft from the bridge. First of all, he would have to tell the radioman to send an SOS.

The faces of Morecliff and Harrington and Davis flashed through his mind. All three had been out there on the fo'c's'le head. One of them knew what was going on, that Clark was certain. But the guilty man was an accomplished actor.

George Davis' face was sharp and cruel. The man was the type that would stop at nothing to gain financial ends.

Of Morecliff, Clark knew little. Of Harrington, he had heard more. The man threw extravagant parties in Havana, was a spendthrift and a lady's man.

At the top of the companionway, Clark stopped and looked forward. Smoke was rolling out from the bridge, dark blotches against the black sky.

The door of the radio room was open, splashing a panel of light out on the dark deck. Clark wondered why the radio operator hadn't spotted the smoke. Great swirls of it were sweeping down upon the place, filling the interior.

Clark coughed and pushed in the screen. Then he stopped. Sprawled across his set, fingers still clutching the key, lay the radioman. One arm hung down toward the floor, blood dripping from the lax fingers. The back of his skull was smashed flat.

Tearing his eyes from the grisly corpse, Clark dived toward another door. Beyond it must be the auxiliary set. The floor was covered with the glass of broken tubes and the main outfit was useless. Throwing back the door, Clark found that the gas engine of the auxiliary set had been smashed. The set itself was hammered to bits. No SOS would go out this night.

A great mass of radiograms was spilled on the floor beside the dead operator. Clark scooped them up, ran through them with trembling fingers. Three he selected. One from Morecliff to New York. One from Davis to Jersey City. One from Harrington to Havana.

His mouth tight and grim, Clark started back toward the salon. In a passageway he came to an abrupt halt. On the floor, beaten to death, lay the steward he had sent to the first officer.

CHAPTER THREE

Groping in the Dark

THE discovery of the white-jacketed body confirmed Clark's suspicions. He was certain now that Davis, Morecliff or Harrington had known his message, or had guessed it.

As he strode down the carpeted passage, the odor of smoke became more noticeable. Clark spotted the first officer in the salon, waving a cocktail glass at a portly gentleman—Harrington.

Oblivious of the eyes which were immediately focused upon him, Clark went straight through the center of the salon to the first mate's table. The officer seemed to sense the nature of the message he was bringing. He set down his glass.

Harrington's eyes seemed to pop out of his fat face. Then another face loomed behind Harrington—the sharp features and black eyes of George Davis. The black eyes were hostile, alive, watchful.

Clark beckoned to the first officer and drew him aside.

"Holt," he said softly, "you're captain of this ship."

Holt blinked and passed a gold-braided sleeve across his eyes.

"What . . . what do you mean? Has anything—"

"The captain is dead, murdered. No one is on the bridge. Your radio is out of working order."

"My God!" jabbered Holt, unnerved.

"And," continued Clark, "you're on fire at sea. Get your crew on the job immediately."

"But who—" began Chief Officer Holt.

"I'll find that out," Clark snapped. "Your job is to get us out of this mess as quickly as possible. I sent a steward to you twenty minutes ago, but he was murdered before he reached you."

Clark spun on his heel and went out. Holt might be unnerved for the moment, but he would know what to do.

Suddenly a small card in the brass holder on a cabin door caught Clark's attention—a card which read "George Davis." Clark glanced back to make certain the corridor was empty. He tried the door. It was unlocked, and he stepped into the cabin.

Grips were stacked against the wall, and beside them lay a briefcase, its contents spilling out on the rug. Clark knelt beside the case and ran quick fingers through the papers. He found several radiograms but they all dealt with market matters.

Then he discovered a series of penciled notations. He was about to pass them by when he saw one figure of a million and a half. Another figure had been subtracted from it, leaving something less than half a million. A million and a half was the value of the dope which had been traced to the dock from which the *Cubana* had sailed.

Clark thrust the paper into his breast pocket and glanced about for other clues.

The knob of the door rattled. Clark jerked to his feet and sprang behind the door, palming his gun.

The door swung back. From behind it, Clark could not see the intruder. There was no other sound. Evidently the person who had entered was standing on the threshold studying the room. Abruptly the door slammed shut, and Clark was again alone.

Quickly he jerked the knob toward him and jumped out into the passageway. A back was retreating around a bend of the corridor. Clark plunged after it. The man ahead was Harrington.

Clark snapped out and caught at the fat man's shoulder, spinning him around. Harrington's face was lined, his eyes wide and fearful.

"What . . . what . . . what's the matter?" he blurted.

"What were you doing in Davis' room?" snapped Clark.

"My wife!" wailed Harrington. "I can't find her. I thought she might . . . might . . . I left her in the cabin twenty minutes ago, and now she's gone."

Clark studied the fat features and then released the shoulder.

"I haven't seen your wife, and I wouldn't know her if I did see her," he informed Harrington. "What were you doing on the fo'c's'le head a half-hour ago?"

"Who, me? Why, I went up there with Davis. He said I'd been drinking too much, needed air. Wanted me to— What are you looking at me that way for, man?"

"Did Davis take you there?" said Clark. "Was he the one that suggested it?"

"Certainly. What's . . . what's wrong with going up there for a minute to get some air? Listen, I've got to find my wife."

"Go ahead," Clark snapped.

Then he walked back toward the salon. Deep in thought, Clark did not at first notice the girl who darted out of a cabin ahead of him. She was tall and blond, well poised, dressed in a flowing evening gown. She glanced back—and her eyes mirrored terror. With two quick strides he caught up with her.

"Pardon me," he offered, "but perhaps I can be of help?"

"Help? Perhaps a moment ago, but not now. We're burning!" Her face was blank, as though she talked in a nightmare. "I saw the smoke, and he's done it!"

"Who's done it?" Clark pursued.

Then she seemed to snap back to reality. She turned as though she wanted to get away, but Clark's gaze held her.

"I don't know who he is," she whispered. "He warned me not to take this boat. He said . . . he said . . ."

"Who are you?" Clark's tone was even, soft. "You are referring to the man who shipped a million and a half dollars' worth of dope on this boat. You are afraid of him for some reason."

She gasped, and looked at him wide-eyed.

"I know nothing about that," came her hasty denial. "I don't want—"

"Don't want him arrested, that it?"

"No, no! I mean—I don't know what I mean! You're a detective. You're ready to pin anything on anybody at the slightest excuse. You won't get her, but I don't care what happens to him. He's rotten all the way through."

"Who is?" demanded Clark.

"I don't know his name. He's a fiend, a devil. He's made

her life a living hell. I only saw him once, and then he wore a mask. His eyes were black and cruel. They bore straight through you. He's aboard this ship. She told me that he was."

"And who is she?"

"Madame Seville, of course."

Clark suppressed his astonishment. Now the ends were beginning to tie together.

"Then Madame Seville is aboard," he pressed. "I have been trying to find her."

"You won't!" declared the girl. "She'll be dead, if she isn't already. I've been searching for an hour, but she has vanished. She was supposed to meet me tonight—to tell me about him—but she didn't come. But if anything happens to me, there are two men that you must watch. One is Morecliff. The other is Davis."

"All right," Clark agreed. "But who are you?"

"I am Harrington's secretary, Jean Raymond."

Leaving the girl in her room, Bob Clark started up the companionway to the boat deck. The smoke which hit him there was blinding, suffocating.

Stepping in close to a funnel, he pulled himself up on a stay and peered forward. Men were up there, scurrying back and forth in the light of the flames, carrying hoses and chemical extinguishers.

By this time, news of the catastrophe was seeping through the cabins. Men and women stood about in huddled little groups, their eyes round with fear, watching the flames.

Morecliff was standing beside a davit looking forward,

a faint smile on his face. His dark eyes swept restlessly, triumphantly, over the scene.

Before Clark could approach him, an elderly lady snatched at the detective's arm.

"Hadn't we better take to the boats?" she cried.

"No," said Clark. "It will be all right in a few minutes, I'm sure. They'll have it all under control."

"But my son says that it's below deck, too!"

Clark left her abruptly. If this were true, it was quite possible that the entire hold would go up in flames. Clark hurried down a companionway and went forward to the deck just under the bridge. He found the shaft. One glance was enough. Far below he could see fire licking.

He jumped to the forward promenade and stared at the first cargo hatch. Small coils of smoke were coming up from the cracks. The hold was on fire. Clark knew in that instant the ship was doomed.

There would be no saving it now. The best they could hope to do would be to send up rocket signals and take to the boats before the deck was consumed.

With that in mind he started in the direction of a companionway, but a small glass case caught his eye. Rockets! With one kick he broke the glass and jerked down an armload.

Stumbling through the haze which now spread from the elevator shaft, Clark made the promenade of B deck. It was completely deserted. He lunged to the rail and threw down his burden. Taking a box of matches from his pocket, he propped a rocket against the rail.

He struck a match, shielded it momentarily from the

whipping wind. Suddenly a hand lashed out and knocked the blaze from his grasp.

The detective whirled, his eye raging. Davis stood there, unperturbed, shaking his head in the negative, a gun in his hand.

"Don't you think that that is the duty of an officer?" he said softly, his hawk face twitching.

"Then get an officer down here!" snapped Clark. His muscles tightened. He measured the distance between them. "Why don't you want me to send out a warning?"

"There are reasons," purred Davis. "I am afraid that I will find it necessary to lock you in your room."

"You tried that once," Clark snapped.

"What do you mean?"

Clark started to shrug, but the movement was deceptive. Suddenly his hands jabbed at the gun. It went off, far to the right. Then his fist smashed into Davis' mouth.

Davis screamed, his black eyes wild with hate. Dropping the gun, he closed in like a madman. Clark stepped aside and snapped another blow to the jaw. Davis wavered—then seemed to go mad.

Shouting wildly, he clawed at Clark's face with talonlike fingers. Viciously he jabbed his knee up toward Clark's groin, but the detective stepped aside.

Clark circled his opponent until the other's back was toward the rail. Avoiding the wild blows with deft sidesteps, the detective's heavy fists beat a relentless tattoo against Davis' face. A left shot home to the point of the jaw—was followed by a stunning right.

Davis tottered, and then slumped inert to the planking. Clark sprang back to the rockets. He lit another match and held the wavering flame to a fuse.

With a sizzling rush, the rocket stabbed up into the night, trailing an arc of fire behind it. A second followed, reached halfway to the zenith before the first exploded with a loud report. The third was the end of the series. At two-minute intervals, Clark sent off the others.

Then Clark dragged the still-unconscious Davis into the salon. Many passengers were there, talking excitedly, their voices husky with fear. Clark found a steward and ordered him to guard Davis. Clark hurried up the companionway to the boat deck. The heat there was terrific. Through the choking smoke, Clark made his way to a lifeboat. To make certain that the boat was in good working order, he pulled himself up on the davit and glanced down into the uncovered hull. Everything seemed all right.

But as he dropped back to the deck, something still troubled him. He turned and grasped the davit, the cranelike arm which was supposed to swing the cutter out over the side so that it could be launched. The davit did not move.

Clark kneeled beside its base. His mouth became hard and set. The joint had been welded tight. The davit could not be moved!

CHAPTER FOUR

"Island Product Samples"

DESPITE the heat which seared his cheeks, Bob Clark stood staring blankly, completely baffled by the puzzle which confronted him. The man who had done this thing would lose a million and a half dollars through it; the dope would be consumed with the ship, a total loss. At the same time, he had trapped himself utterly by rendering these lifeboats useless.

Was he a senseless fool? Clark did not think so. There was something else in back of all this.

Harrington, face lit up with anxiety, came reeling through the smoke and jostled against Clark.

"Have you found my wife?"

"I wasn't looking for your wife," Clark told him. "Have you been in the reading rooms and the salons?"

"All of them!" cried Harrington, suddenly unmanned. "All of them! She's gone, and we're sinking! We'll die, all of us, like rats! Why don't they take to the boats? Why don't these officers do something?"

"Quiet," admonished Clark. "You'll start a panic."

"Panic! Panic! What do I care for that? She's gone, and they're letting us die!"

Harrington's bloated features quivered with grief. He

staggered away, lurching drunkenly, blinded by smoke and tears.

Clark started forward to find Holt. The chief mate was black and disheveled, sweating with a hose line.

"The pumps are petering out on us," he wailed. "There isn't any steam in the lines. That damned engineer—"

"You'll have steam," snapped Clark.

He whirled and started down the companionway toward amidships, intending to head for the engine room, but the sight of Morecliff stopped him. Morecliff was standing in the background, watching the losing fight against the flames. Clark heard the man laugh. He grabbed Morecliff by the shoulder and spun him about.

"You've been getting a big kick out of this, haven't you?" Clark rasped. "What's so funny about it?"

"Why, I . . . I . . . you see, I have some tankers; and the West Indies Lines—" Morecliff fell silent and sagged back. And then, suddenly, his fist swept up in a vicious arc, but Clark had been watching for just that move. He jabbed a fast right into the oil man's throat, and sent him back gasping, screaming.

"Damn you!" roared Morecliff. "I'll get you, you lousy dick!"

He pawed at his thigh, fumbling for a gun. Clark kicked the weapon away. Morecliff went limp, and Clark left him where he lay.

Still boiling, Clark swung into the passageway on B deck and headed toward the stern. He went into the salon and found the place deserted.

George Davis was nowhere in evidence, nor was the steward

with whom Clark had left him. What did that mean? Clark determined to find out.

A light footfall in back of him caused him to whirl around. The girl, Jean Raymond, was hurrying toward him. Anxiety was written on her beautiful features. Her dress was in tatters.

"I can't find her!" she cried. "But I found something else. I have been looking everywhere for you."

"You mean you can't find Madame Seville?" said Clark.

"No, but I found this." She extended a slip of paper, the shipper's copy of a bill of lading. "I thought it might be a code message or something."

"Where did this come from?" demanded Clark.

"It was lying under George Davis' door when I went in there the second time."

Clark stared at it. It was an ordinary bill of lading, not at all remarkable save for the cubic footage it covered. This, however, immediately aroused Clark's interest. He calculated that a million and a half dollars' worth of heroin would occupy just about that space. The bill was marked "Island Product Samples." A notation showed that the goods were to be stowed in hold Number Four, all the way aft.

Sending the girl forward, Clark swung down a ladder which was marked "Engine Room." He came to a huge double door of steel and swung it open. Below him lay the ship's engines.

He swung down three stages and looked forward. Far below, on the engine room floor, he spied a huddled form. Otherwise, the place was deserted. That was why they were getting no steam on the upper deck.

Then Clark saw the flames. They leaped out from the

bulkhead and licked at a shining turbine. Though there was nothing there to burn, the fire was sweeping on down the steel floor. The oil tanks! They had been pierced and then set afire.

Undecided for an instant, Clark hovered on the ladder. If he went aft to trace that dope, he might be trapped in the hold; the fire was sweeping straight down upon it.

For a moment his shoes beat a rapid tattoo on the iron rungs; then he reached a decision. He was going down! The blaze leaped out at him like a hungry beast. He snatched at a rail and slid to the next stage. Under his feet the steel plates were like the top of a stove.

Running swiftly around the mighty engines, he made his way to a double door and dashed through. It was still hot here, but not as bad as it had been in the engine room. This passage led to the hold.

Far aft, Clark found another door, and went through it to the sparsely filled Number Four. The lights were still burning, running on emergency batteries. He could see the piles of boxes.

Without difficulty, he found the boxes marked "Island Product Samples." They were quite innocent in appearance, extremely light. Clark smashed the first down against the plates. Then he took a second, a third, a fourth.

Abruptly he jerked to his feet, swearing. Every box was empty! He had found no dope. The lead which had brought him to the *Cubana* was evidently false. But it had looked so certain, had been so pat!

Face set, he plunged again for the open air, to burst out onto a deck where all hell had broken loose. The panic-stricken passengers had thrown off all restraint. They were tearing at each other, fighting to get at the boats, leaping overboard.

The fire had consumed the deckhouses now. It was reaching down into the cabins. Flame spouted everywhere. The terrific heat became unbearable.

Bitterly Clark cursed the man responsible for this horror. Grimly he swore to apprehend the fiend somehow.

Morecliff was staggering aft, fighting dully to get down the companionway. Harrington was pleading with the third officer to find his wife. Davis was nowhere to be seen.

And then Clark heard a new sound—the sputter of an engine. He ran down a companionway to the deck below, and there to the rail. Dimly seen by the red glow of the fire, a launch lay hard in under the *Cubana*'s bows. Clark watched it with hard eyes.

Some of the mystery was explained by the presence of that boat. It was a seagoing craft, very fast, and had undoubtedly come out straight from the shore. But its furtiveness showed that it had not come in response to the signal rockets.

A dim shadow appeared at the ship's rail above the launch. The shadow was holding a flashlight. The light blinked twice in rapid succession.

From the cockpit of the boat came an answering blink. Clark's .38 stabbed out redly before him. The light in the boat went out. Above the bedlam of shouts around him, Clark heard a scream. The shadow at the rail faltered. A red tongue of flame suddenly illuminated the man's face. It was masked! Clark fired again, and the shadow disappeared.

Clark grabbed a life preserver rope, tied one end to the rail, and went over the side in a clean dive. When he reached the rope's end, the jerk almost pulled his arms from their sockets, but he swung toward the bobbing boat. On the first arc he let go and caught at the rail as he went by.

"Who's that?" snarled a voice in the cockpit.

"Some crazy loon. Shoot him!" another directed.

But Clark shot first. The second man to speak clutched at his chest and tumbled over the side. The first jerked out a gun and fired straight at the face above the rail. Again, the .38 won. His face stinging from the burned powder, Clark climbed up over the side and dropped into the pit.

The launch was more than seventy-five feet in length, powered by heavy, throbbing Diesels. Clark went straight to the wheelhouse. A head thrust itself out.

"Who's that? The boss?" a heavy voice demanded.

Before Clark could answer, a flashlight outlined him. Clark shot just over the top of it. There was a grunt. He fired again. The flashlight rolled down the sloping planks and splashed into the sea.

Warily, the Federal man entered the wheelhouse. The thing he wanted was on the charting table—a radio with all tubes burning. Although the set was small, it would be sufficient.

He sat down before the key and hammered out a test phrase. The set responded. Then the key pounded out the first news that the outside world was to hear of the *Cubana* disaster.

"SOS . . . SOS," chattered the key. "SOS . . . calling all ships on the high seas. SS *Cubana* in flames about fifty miles off the coast of New Jersey. No lifeboats, pumps failed. All ships rush aid immediately."

Then Clark shut off the set and went out on deck. With cupped hands he bawled for Holt.

"Send down an officer and crew for this launch!" he shouted, when the chief mate appeared at the rail. "I've sent an SOS. You can use this to pick the people out of the water."

They threw him a line and he wrapped it around an iron bitt. Every nerve in his body urged him to stay there next to the cool water. But he had to go back up into that hell to get the man who was responsible for it. Hand over hand, Clark went up the rope. In a moment the deck was scorching his feet.

That deck was an inferno of terrified people. Through the milling mass, Clark saw Harrington. The man's fat face was drawn with agony.

"We're lost!" he shouted, when he spied Clark. "We'll all die!"

"Help is on the way," Clark said, as levelly as possible. "Buck up. Did you find your wife?"

Harrington stared at him with unseeing eyes and shook his head vaguely as Clark strode away, his searching eyes darting to the right and left. He located a steward and grabbed the fellow by his white jacket.

"What was the number of Harrington's room?" he shouted.

"Suite B-6," the white-clad figure gasped.

Clark took off his wet coat and wrapped it about his face. He stumbled toward a smoke-filled companionway, and went down haltingly. He felt as though he walked through a blast furnace. As he stared forward, the fire lashed at him, driving him back. He buried his face deeper in the coat and plunged ahead.

B-6 was a raging furnace. The woodwork had been consumed and the terrific heat had all but melted the metal.

Clark plunged inside, gritting his teeth. He groped about on the floor until his fingers encountered something soft and yielding. Dragging at it, he retreated swiftly, the passageway collapsing behind him as he went. Shouldering his burden, he staggered up the companionway.

Clark threw down the charred body beside the forward mast and, shielding his face against the wall of flame which came from the bridge, looked about for Harrington. It was several minutes before he found the fat man and led him to the mast. Harrington seemed devoid of all intelligence; he had given up.

"Is that your wife?" Clark pointed down at the body.

The face was black, the flesh charred. There was little left for identification except a necklace of gold. Harrington fumbled with the locket. Then he stared up at Clark, his eyes unseeing.

"Yes," he croaked, and then collapsed over the body.

Clark dragged him away. Harrington stood up, finally, and Clark shoved him against an iron bitt and told him to stay there. Then Clark made his way aft. He had not seen Morecliff. Nor had he seen Davis. He meant to find them, especially Davis.

The heat was beyond human endurance. Close to the bridge, the air would sear the lungs, would kill instantly. Then the forward hatch blew off, and a geyser of flame leaped to the height of the mast.

Try as he would, Clark could not get within fifty feet of the passageways.

CHAPTER FIVE

The Firebug

IT was two o'clock in the morning before the first rescue ship loomed up out of the haze beside the *Cubana*. Clark went to the rail and stared at the newcomer with seared eyes.

"What's at the bottom of all this?" the second mate beside him asked wearily. "I don't know who you are, but you seem to be in the know."

"Not yet, I'm not," said Clark. "Do you know Morecliff when you see him?"

"Sure, but I haven't seen him for an hour. He's a big shot in the oil game up north. Runs a line out of Venezuela—tankers. He lost one of his contracts, and he had to lay off a lot of his boats. He was pretty sore about it. I wonder why he took this ship."

"And how about George Davis?" Clark pursued.

"Haven't seen him for a while either. He's kind of nutty. He's on the board of this line. This loss will cost them plenty."

"What about insurance?" asked Clark.

"Oh, there may be plenty of that." The officer peered intently at the detective. "Say—you don't think they tried to burn us for the insurance, do you? The line has been running in a hole for three years now. I'll—"

He gripped the rail to steady himself. Clark caught him and

kept him from falling. He dragged him up into the extreme bow and propped him up against a winch.

The wall of heat was like a savage advancing army. All the cabins were going now. The sea glowed as red as blood all about the blazing pyre.

Morecliff staggered up, stumbling, his face drawn with fear and exhaustion. Clark eased him to the deck and kneeled beside him. Then, certain that Morecliff would live, the Federal man crawled aft closer to the flames. His red-rimmed eyes peered everywhere for Davis.

Lying in the protection of a bitt, Clark found him. Gasping for breath, his bladelike face swollen and blistered, Davis looked up with dull eyes. There was something unnatural about the man's attitude. His back looked stiff, as though braced against pain.

"A knife," croaked Davis. "He got . . . me . . . with a knife. He . . ."

The man had fainted. Clark rolled him over. The hilt of a weapon protruded from between his shoulder blades. Clark pulled it out. Thrusting a handful of kapok taken from a torn lifebelt over the wound, he bound it as well as he could.

Then, suddenly, he felt his head swimming—and the deck was hot against his cheek. He could no longer find the strength to hold up his head. He realized that he had been running on sheer nerve for hours, and now that nerve was gone.

Twice he tried to stagger to the rail, where the rescue liner's boats were dragging people from the water. But it was no use. He was too tired to go on—too tired to fight. . . .

"*Cubana,* ahoy!" a loud, bellowing voice rolled out across

the water. "Coast Guard cutter 337! Stand by with lines! We'll take you off!"

Robert W. Clark, of the US Secret Service, sat up. It was as though he had had a bucket of ice water thrown over his scorched body. The Coast Guard! His own outfit!

On his feet, he found a line. Found a monkey fist and threw it round and round his head. It whistled away from him. He felt it jerk tight. Then he began to pull. A hawser was coming toward him. A man gave him a hand.

The hawser was dropped over the bitt. A winch on the cutter creaked and whirred. It was coming right in alongside the *Cubana*.

Person after person went over to the cutter to be treated for burns and exposure—out of the red hell to the cool 'tween decks of the gray ship.

Now other vessels were arriving, and the sea was laced with crisscrossing searchlights.

But not until dawn did Bob Clark allow himself to stagger into the cutter's sick bay for treatment, hot coffee and, better than either, sleep.

Hours later, with the afternoon sun pouring through the wardroom ports of the cutter, Bob Clark was finishing his story of the disaster. Only a few officials were there, and a few of the passengers of the doomed *Cubana*. Davis, Morecliff and Harrington sat against the far wall under guard. Jean Raymond looked across the green-covered table at Bob Clark.

"Now," said Clark, "to finish up, I promised to tell you who the firebug is, and why he did it. I know now that none of all this was without reason. The man was driven by fear and greed."

He spread out the three radiograms he had taken from the radio room, the ace of spades, the gold locket, the bill of lading.

"These will give us the entire story. I thought for a while that all this was caused by Davis. But it was not. Actually, Davis is a dupe. Head of the most powerful drug ring in New York, he ordered a million and a half dollars' worth of dope from Havana. He paid a million in advance, leaving the other half million to be paid on delivery. I found the notation of these amounts in Davis' briefcase. This bill of lading was discovered on Davis' stateroom floor. You will notice that Davis is the consignee."

Heads nodded. All eyes were fastened on Clark.

"Davis, as director of this company, was able to import dope without inspection. He made good use of the fact that no one would ever suspect him." Clark glanced at Davis' contorted face. "He thought that this dope was contained in these boxes, but he had nothing to do with the fire. I thought he had, when he interfered with my sending rockets. I know now that, as an officer of the line, he did not want another ship to salvage on the *Cubana* before it was absolutely necessary. He did not know how bad the fire actually was.

"As for Morecliff, he was glad about the fire until it threatened his own life. He was sore because the West Indies Lines took business away from him. Therefore, Harrington is the firebug—the murderer!"

Harrington's fat form lurched out of the chair. An automatic pushed him back.

"Harrington received the dope order from Davis. Harrington handles dope from South America and relays it to the United States. Harrington is greedy, and a coward. He received that million dollars with which he was supposed to purchase heroin and opium. He spent it and could not replace it—and he had no dope. He was afraid of Davis—terribly afraid of what Davis would do to him if the dope was not actually aboard. Unknown to Davis, those boxes were empty, and there was no dope aboard the *Cubana*.

"Now get this. Harrington had to cover up that fact before Davis discovered it. Therefore the *Cubana* had to be destroyed. So Harrington arranged to have a launch trail the liner. He thought he would be able to get away on it, but I happened along in time to spike that plan. Harrington wanted the *Cubana* to sink or burn. Fire was easier to handle. So he set fire to the liner by means of an acetylene torch connected with the bell hammer of the captain's clock.

"At eight bells, the clock opened the valve of the acetylene tank, and the fire began. Harrington had an alibi. He made certain that Davis and Morecliff were on the fo'c's'le head with him at eight bells.

"Then, so that no word could be sent out, Harrington murdered the radio operator and smashed the set. So that the ship would go off her course and lose her position, making her hard to locate, he killed the bridge officer and the helmsman. To make certain that no witness against him could escape, he had welded the bottoms of the lifeboat davits so that none of the boats could be launched.

"Harrington knew a Narcotics man was aboard. He had

made certain that this fake dope cargo was traced in Havana; he wanted Davis to be sure that dope was aboard and that he, Harrington, had not swindled Davis. Afraid that the Narcotics man would gum his plans, he tortured the captain into revealing my name. Then he tried several times to kill me.

"When Harrington knew that he was slipping up, he started howling about his wife. There was a corpse in his cabin, but it was not his wife's. This locket from the dead woman's neck says, 'To Madame Seville, for past services and future loyalty.' Madame Seville was an aide of Harrington's. But he knew she was double-crossing him. This ace of spades was written on by the dying captain, naming Madame Seville as the dope runner.

"Jean Raymond and Madame Seville worked together. Jean Raymond was not certain that Harrington was the head of the Havana ring, but she had her ideas. Madame Seville was going to make the revelation last night, but she died before she got a chance.

"Harrington was ironbound in his alibis. He couldn't have started the fire, but he did. He wouldn't destroy a million and a half in dope, and so he knew that that would never be suspected by those who knew of his dope activities. And he wouldn't kill his wife. But Harrington's wife was in Havana. He sent her this radiogram on the night before the fire. I found it. That tripped up Harrington.

"As for other angles of the case, I gave Davis into the hands of the steward, who immediately released him because Davis was a company director. Davis was stabbed by Harrington

72

just before we were rescued, because Harrington was afraid Davis would get wise. But he failed that time.

"And finally, I want to get an invitation to Harrington's execution. I'm not bloodthirsty, but he ought to be burned a thousand times for that flaming hell he kindled for innocent people!"

Then Clark pulled a piece of paper toward him and scribbled out his report to his chief in Washington:

There was no dope on the *Cubana*.
(Signed) Robert W. Clark

KILLER APE

KILLER APE

BILL LACY was the kind of newspaperman who would go to a nice murder and come back with a lead story about a run-over dog.

But human interest and animals were the things which brought Bill Lacy low the night the corpse was found on Forest Road.

All unsuspecting, he swung down the dingy corridor of the precinct station, whistling to himself and at peace with the world.

He bumped squarely into Captain O'Connor who scowled like an evil genie. O'Connor had not much use for tall, brown-haired men of handsome visage, as O'Connor was quite the reverse.

"Watch where you're goin'," snapped O'Connor.

"Oh, beg pardon," said Bill with a wicked grin. "You startled me for a moment. I thought it was King Kong."

"Blah!" snarled O'Connor. "You still harpin' on apes!"

Sergeant Morris had come along, waddling sourly. "Apes? Is this sap still talkin' about apes? Still protectin' your relatives, Lacy?"

"Look," said Bill, "you guys lay off me about that ape stuff. All I did was sock that guy Hartman for . . ."

"For being crooel to a pore little monkey," said O'Connor.

"Orangutan," corrected Bill. "And I still think it's a damned shame the way Para Rubber Company and Hartman, just for the sake of outselling Greyson, put poor Joe . . ."

"In a cage," said Sergeant Morris. "Poor Joe, the orangutan! He ought to be wearin' a silk hat and swingin' a cane. Aw, we read the papers, Bill. We read what you wrote about poor old Joe, hardly able to stand up in his cage. . . ."

"And we locked you up when you socked Hartman," said O'Connor. "And if you don't stop pannin' the police every time something happens, you're going to be locked up again—plenty of times. Get that?"

"Keep your badge on," said Bill. "If I want to write a sob story about an abused ape . . ."

A radio operator came out of his stall like Punch. "Hey, Cap, I heard you. That ape was let out about an hour ago. Hartman just phoned and I'm sending Car Eighteen up to escort him out of the building. He's scared. Yah," he added to Bill and vanished.

O'Connor looked at Bill. "Say, Mr. Lacy, it wouldn't be that you let yourself go on this idea, would you? Where you been?"

"Me?" gaped Bill. "Why, walkin' around in the snow . . ."

"Huh," said O'Connor. "Pretty thin! What's the idea stealin' an ape? It didn't belong to you! Even if Hartman was abusin' it, it was his ape! Now you come along and . . ."

"Cap!" said the operator, popping out again. "Woman out on Forest Road reports that she seen an ape running down in the woods."

"In the snow?" said Bill. "Nuts. Joe wouldn't go out in the snow. He's from Sumatra. . . ."

"Call Car Twenty and tell them to watch for him," said Captain O'Connor. "Say, how could he get from Para Rubber to Forest Road in an hour? That's miles! And through the downtown traffic and somebody would have spotted him. Say, Lacy, what is this? You tryin' to . . ."

"Cap!" yelped the operator, popping out again. "He's done it! He's gone and murdered somebody. A motorist just phoned in to say that he seen a corpse alongside Forest Road in the ditch. Get Homicide Squad here and which medical examiner . . ."

O'Connor grabbed too late. Bill was already vanishing in wild flight down the front steps. But before the door banged shut, O'Connor bawled, "Come back here, damn you! You're an accessory to murder!"

Bill wasn't waiting to be an accessory to anything except his car.

He raced down the steps, skidding on the icy walks now covered with sleet. He leaped into his coupe and thanked God the engine was still warm. He crashed gears and rocketed out into the street, headed for Forest Road.

The ride was long and he had plenty of time to think. Maybe Joe had gotten out and had gone mad or something. Maybe Hartman had done something to make him mad. Maybe Joe would attack anybody on sight!

He passed the last of the city filling stations and clattered over a bridge toward a strip of woods. Gradually he slowed down so that he could divide his attention between driving and watching, and was then forced to decrease his speed even further. At this slower pace, the snow did not pile so heavily against his windshield and the wiper started to work with a will.

A half a mile went slowly by and then Bill saw what he had been looking for. He had turned a corner in the white road and his headlights struck squarely on something which lay sacklike and still on the edge of a drift. Bill pulled cautiously over to the side and stopped.

When his motor died he sat for some seconds looking at the dark shape. There was no mistaking its identity. It was a corpse. The face lay buried, but there was something about the arms which made Bill's heart drum against his ribs in rising tempo. Though long a reporter, Bill had always shivered at the sight of a dead man.

At last he opened the door and got out. The snow covered the low-cut oxfords and found holes in his coat through which to drive. It was cold, and out here where the wind had no other resistance than trees, Bill Lacy had to lean against it to proceed. The leafless branches overhead moaned out a dirge. Stepping carefully without marring the tracks, Bill went to the side of the dead man. He didn't touch it, for that was a job for the police. He merely stood there and looked down and tried to bring himself to realize that old Joe had had a hand in it.

The head, though partially covered by the drifting sleet, was bent at an angle which told the story of a broken neck. The hands—hands which would never feel anything again—clutched stiffly at the white ground. The skin was an ugly blue, visible even in this poor light.

Bill Lacy's lips were tight when he struggled back to the car. For a moment he was half-minded to jump in and leave the scene before some unforeseen nemesis cut him down. But instead he reached into a side pocket and pulled out a flashlight.

Back again across the road, Bill didn't turn his beam on the corpse. He was shivery enough already without looking at that thing again. He picked out marks which looked like barefoot tracks and went ahead into the denseness of the thickets.

At first he had been certain of one thing—that he and Joe were friends. But now that feeling began to inch away with the warmth of his body. He had had the idea that if he didn't get out here and save Joe from the cops, he'd curse himself for the rest of his life. He knew they'd shoot Joe on sight, for Joe's appearance was against him. Long arms, an ugly face. Sure, some rookie would spot him and drill him through the skull in a minute.

Bill Lacy's hands lost their warmth to the cold barrel of the flashlight and the snow crept down into his shoes until he could feel the water squish each time he stepped. He wore light, unlined gloves and as the sleet melted upon them, they became wet. The makers of his overcoat had cut the collar too low and he could feel his ears grow chilly pink.

But the barefoot tracks drifted out ahead of him, deeper and deeper, into the wood. Because he was cold himself, Bill was sympathizing with Joe. It must be tough, walking barefoot through these drifts, and Joe had been born down there near the equator where the sun was hot.

The tracks went around in a curve and came back. Bill found where the orangutan had stood for some little time behind a tree as though waiting. The snow was tramped down on the spot and melted. Bill stood for several seconds looking at the marks. He was suddenly gripped by shivers which were not traceable to the coldness of the night. Joe had stood there with his feet apart waiting and crouching, ready to spring. Only the toe marks were plainly visible. Yes, Joe had been waiting to spring.

Ahead along the wandering trail stood other trees. Trees which were larger and could more securely hide an ape from view. Bill looked at them, his eyes questioning. He did not trust his logic then. He knew that Joe expected pursuit and that Joe was waiting for it. He knew that Joe—yes, there was no evading it now—would kill to get away.

Bill shivered again and looked behind him. Not until now had he realized how alone he was and how little protection he had against a pair of great hairy hands which could in an instant snuff out his life. Even if he and Joe were still friends—well, maybe Joe wouldn't know who it was until it was too late.

Overhead the wind moaned on, sighing an accompaniment to the silent, relentless sleet.

"Joe!" shouted the newspaperman, and immediately wished he hadn't spoken. His voice sounded too hollow and fantastic in all this loneliness. Besides, Joe wasn't a dog. He wouldn't come like a dog if you called him. Joe was a great, hunched brute who stood up and placed his knuckles on the ground. As he shot it about, the beam of his flashlight was hampered by the falling flakes. He was half-hoping now that he wouldn't find the orangutan. He didn't feel up to seeing Joe dart out from the ambush of a white-mantled tree.

Bill Lacy squared his shoulders and went on. The barefoot tracks were going straight ahead now, and he thought that there was less snow drifted into each successive print. No use giving up. Some rookie would blow Joe's head off his shoulders before Joe could move. The orangutan's appearance was against him.

And then Bill stopped as though held by a wall. He shot the beam of his light up toward the place where he had caught a glint of green fire. He stood with his feet spread apart, looking up the trail, trying to overcome the sudden inertia of his body.

Joe stood there beside a tree, blinking in the harsh white light. And Joe's lips were frothed with reddish foam. His arms went down to the ground and he held himself into the sleet by pressing his knuckles against the snow. His hair was matted with the melting flakes and his teeth gleamed whitely against the brownish black of his lips. His teeth were long, too long. The wind was carrying the man scent to him.

Bill Lacy overcame the shock of his discovery. He told himself that this was just Joe, the orangutan—and the lonesome orangutan at that—who had been his friend. He started to call out to the brute, but the words stuck in his chilled throat.

Joe stood there beside a tree, blinking in the harsh white light.
And Joe's lips were frothed with reddish foam.

Foam was dripping from Joe's teeth. It was plain that the ape was mad.

And then Joe began to hunch himself forward. His flat face was without expression, but his eyes, gazing into that blinding beam, were slitted and somehow terrifying. The arms, twice the length and three times the strength of a man's, were taut as though expectant of a fight.

Bill Lacy turned away. His legs were staggering underneath him and his eyes were suddenly shot with the hideous knowledge of his situation. Joe had gone mad and had broken loose. He'd broken one man's neck and now—well, now Bill Lacy was here with a killer ape, alone with him in a lonely forest.

And Bill Lacy ran. He couldn't stop himself once he had started. All the terror of the night which had accumulated within him burst its bounds and made a red haze in front of his eyes. He was sprinting and it seemed to him that his racing feet did not touch the snow. He was running toward the road, darting in and out between the trees.

Once he looked back and risked a fall by shooting his beam along his trail. The five-foot orangutan was hunching along on all fours, jaws still foaming. As he looked, Bill heard the brute grunt loudly. Almost two hundred pounds of death was matching speed with the pursued.

And again Bill ran, even faster. He didn't know that he had lost his soft felt hat. He didn't know that his shoes were crammed with snow. He only knew that if he stopped, he would be crushed and broken in the powerful arms of a brute gone mad.

When his first terror had paled through his growing weariness, Bill turned at right angles to his trail and raced along for a hundred yards. He snapped out the light and dodged in between the dim, moaning shapes of giant trees. He went on for some distance before he stopped.

His breath was coming with harsh gasps, but he stilled the sound. He could run no longer without a rest, and he hoped against hope that he would be able to get away before the orangutan spotted him again.

He could hear nothing above the wind and the whisper of sleet and though his finger itched against the button of his light he forced himself to remain in the dark. Some sound would tell him when the brute came too close.

He waited until the beating of his heart grew less. Out there the mad orangutan was hunting for him, trying to find him so that he could be the victor of a second fight against man. Once more Bill Lacy saw the vision of that huddled body along the road.

And then the snow crunched close at hand and Bill Lacy was once more running. He snapped on the light and shot it behind him and saw that the brute was still coming.

The newspaperman wove his way among the grim trees and kept his course, as nearly as he could judge, toward the road. The limbs here were too high to offer a tree-road for the ape, and Bill was thankful for that at least. Apes could travel like the wind in trees.

Ahead was a shallow gully, scarcely more than a shadow against the bluish white carpet. Bill Lacy saw it, but misjudged its depth. He went through the brittle willows at its edge expecting to cross the obstruction in a short leap. But the snow was crusted and an oxford went through. Bill tripped and sprawled through space. His head was down when he struck the soft bottom, but that didn't save his ankle, and when he tried to struggle to his feet he found that he couldn't stand. With a grunt he sank down and shut off his light. It was impossible to go far on a twisted ankle.

Through the whisper of sleet and the low sigh of the wind he tried to catch the sound of the running ape. He knew that the warning would do him little good for he was a helpless prisoner, trapped by a damaged foot. He would have to lie there and wait for death to overtake him. Bill Lacy had never felt so all alone.

A shadow came and stood on the rim of the gully, looking down. A shadow which was five feet tall and whose arms reached down to the snow-packed ground. The orangutan stood still for several seconds.

Under that scrutiny, something in Bill Lacy snapped. He tried to struggle up to his feet, but the ankle wobbled and let him down again. Sick with apprehension, he did not even feel the pain of his effort. Helplessly he lay back and threw his arms across his face.

The ape was struggling down through the willows and the snow was crunching harshly under his heavy weight. Bill heard it, but couldn't bring himself to look up. In an instant those arms would go around his neck, he'd feel bristly hair against his face and that would be the end of the world for him.

Sniffing filled the night about him. He caught the strong smell of the ape as it circled him. Occasionally he could feel the brush of an arm against his rigid body. Time was standing still. Once or twice, Bill attempted to cry out, but the effort caught in his tight throat. No use of that. It would merely enrage the brute.

And then a low sigh came to him. Something was trying to lift a corner of his tight-buttoned overcoat. A great, shaggy body was pressing against him—gently.

Bill Lacy was incredulous that he was still alive. Cautiously he stretched out a wet hand and felt of Joe's matted shoulder. And Joe reached up with a long, black hand and pulled Bill's arm around him.

Reaction caused the newspaperman's chest to heave in silent laughter. No sound passed his lips, for he was still too taut for that. Instead he lay there in the silence of the whispering sleet and shook with racking chuckles. It was not for some minutes that he found his own voice.

"What's the matter, Joe?" asked Lacy. "Did you get cold?"

For answer Joe pressed tight against him and tried once more to crawl under Bill's overcoat. He grunted a great ape grunt.

So that was it. Joe had smelled him downwind and had given pursuit in the hope his friend could do something for him. And after all, why not? Bill had found durian nuts for Joe to eat and Bill had been the only one who saw something besides a curiosity beneath Joe's shaggy hide.

Bill touched Joe's mouth and then turned the flashlight on his fingers. He saw the reddish foam clustering there, but no alarm was in it now. He examined Joe's lips and found that several cuts were in prominence.

"Got hacked up, somehow, didn't you, old boy? I wonder..."
But whatever Lacy wondered about was suddenly silenced
by a pain which shot up his leg.

The newspaperman unbuttoned his overcoat, though that
meant exposing his own chest to the sleet, and passed a corner
of it around the orangutan's shoulders. And then, using Joe
as a handhold, Bill managed to get up.

Painfully, he pulled off the offending shoe and inspected
his chilled ankle. He moved it back and forth and discovered
to his vast relief that it was only a slight sprain. He took his
silk scarf and wound it tightly about the joint, giving it a
measure of support.

Joe pressed close against him and watched intently, and
then Joe inspected his own feet. The gesture made Bill smile
until he remembered that Joe's feet were bare and that snow
is a cold thing.

Forgetting his own ailments, Bill Lacy took a great handful
of flakes and began rubbing Joe's cold right foot. Joe chattered
at him and tried to push the white stuff away, giving the
newspaperman looks which held great, but mock, rage. And
Bill, rubbed on until he thought the circulation had been
restored. After that he gave Joe's other foot a like treatment.

Bill shucked off his overcoat and then his suit coat, utterly
disregarding the fact that the night was bitter. He took the
suit coat and made Joe put it on. It was not a new coat, and
even if it was, he couldn't have Joe catching pneumonia and
dying on him. Back in his car there was a pint flask of whiskey.
He'd make Joe take on some of that.

At the thought of his own coupe, Bill remembered that

O'Connor and Morris, and perhaps Hartman would soon be on the spot if they weren't already. And if they were, Joe would be shot down on sight. Bill didn't want that to happen. If Joe had choked a man to death it had probably occurred through ample provocation, and apes didn't have any knowledge of the law codes. Besides, Joe was entitled to some sort of a trial.

Bill decided to let the problem of getting Joe back to town intact take care of itself. He bent his efforts to making Joe as weatherproof as possible. With this in mind, Bill put his spare oxford on Joe's right foot, and Joe didn't seem to mind. Evidently that little girl down in Oleleh, Sumatra, had often indulged in the sport of dressing her pet orangutan. Around the left foot Bill wrapped his silk handkerchief.

Joe gave him an occasional questioning glance out of his great brown eyes, but it was evident that anything Bill wanted to do was all right with Joe. The ape's face looked incredibly old and incredibly wise, and his red hair, standing straight up above his black face, made Bill think of an ancient Irishman. All Joe needed was a pipe and a "begorrah" between his teeth.

And then they were ready to travel. Bill placed an arm across the ape's shoulders and made Joe understand that he had to walk toward the road, and by making Joe bear all the weight which rightfully belonged to Bill's right foot, they made fairly rapid progress.

They had gone perhaps three hundred yards through the filtering sleet when Bill heard the muffled sound of a shot.

"The cops," said Bill. "Shooting at shadows and scared to death."

That meant that they would have to reach the road below

the position of the body, cross it and come upon the coupe from the other side. Bill didn't quite know what he meant to do, but he did know that he wouldn't let Joe be shot down in cold blood. Even if Joe had killed a man there must have been ample provocation. Bill told himself that over and over, and Joe, lurching steadily along with an amiable grunt here and there, hardly put him in mind of a murderer. Besides, Bill Lacy had an idea about this thing.

Bill placed no blame on the orangutan for the sprained ankle, for it was not like Bill to blame animals for things they couldn't help. Instead, Bill thanked the night that he had Joe there to help him back to his car. Otherwise he would have had to crawl.

An occasional shot sounded in the trees but none of them were even close. Bill surmised—and rightly—that nobody would think to follow Joe's trail. That trail would be covered by drifting snow and countless other prints by this time. The woods were swarming with police who carried their revolvers at full cock.

At last they came to the road and felt the concrete under the rutty snow. No police had come down this far, and evidently no searching parties were at work on the other side. In a moment they had entered the woods and were again out of sight.

The wind was coming down the road to them and now Joe stopped in a listening attitude. His great nostrils quivered and his sniffs were gruff.

"What's up?" asked Bill.

But Joe merely sniffed again and then started on in the

direction Bill wanted to go. Occasionally, Joe sent a slit-eyed glance toward the source of the man odor.

As they approached their destination, Bill swore at himself for placing the car so close to the obvious headquarters of the police. If they spotted Joe, they'd shoot in spite of anything he could do. And Bill didn't want Joe to die.

The newspaperman made Joe slow down and Joe seemed to sense some of the alarm which beat in Bill's heart. The ape stopped now and then to test the wind and for him it seemed to carry great warning.

Lights flickered ahead of them through the trees, making the gaunt branches stand out spectrally against the white. Bill could see his coupe and sighed when he ascertained that no one stood within a hundred feet of it. If they walked silently, he could smuggle Joe into the car without being seen.

Scraps of conversation were coming to them, but they had no meaning for Bill. One thing at a time. Together the pair crept in closer to the coupe.

At last Bill steered the ape into the covering shelter of the car and stopped for a moment, listening. Joe's great nostrils quivered and his jaws flecked out bits of foam.

Bill opened the coupe door and made Joe climb in. Joe hoisted himself up on the seat, and then with an intelligence which was startling, hunched himself down out of sight.

"That's a good boy," whispered Bill.

The pint was in the side pocket where it had lain for such emergencies and Bill brought it out and took a small swallow. Joe watched him and reached for it. Debating for a brief moment the wisdom of giving the ape strong drink, Bill decided that drunkenness was preferable to pneumonia and handed the bottle over.

Whatever Joe had expected the bottle to contain, he made no objections now. He took a large swallow and coughed. With great care he handed the bottle back to his friend.

"Stay right there," whispered Bill. "I'll be back."

And then Bill Lacy took a notch on his nerve and forced himself to walk into the crowd. O'Connor saw him, gaped and then snatched at his arm. "Okay, wise guy. Now who's holding aces?"

"Hands off," said Bill. "If I'm wrong you can arrest me and if I'm right I'm free. You got to give me a chance. I can't get away now."

Doubtfully, O'Connor scowled at him. "You know something? You know where that damned ape is?"

"Maybe," said Bill. And he sat down on the running board of a police car to ease his ankle while Morris stood guard over him.

The coroner was there with two others of his staff, and police were in great evidence. Three newshawks, one of Bill's *Star*, stood around staring into the shadows in case the ape showed up. In the headlights their breath was like cigarette smoke.

And then Bill Lacy saw Hartman, president of Para Rubber. Hartman was not beating his arms or stamping his feet. He was gazing into the woods with fear-widened eyes.

"Hello, Hartman," said Bill and saw Hartman jump. "I wouldn't be afraid of Joe if I were you. I don't think he'd hurt anybody."

Hartman looked at the still corpse and laughed harshly. "No? I suppose he was playing with this poor devil."

O'Connor, glaring at Bill, snapped, "Keep out of this, jailbird. You can't save your own neck by fogging this up!"

"Maybe I know something," said Bill.

O'Connor looked doubtful again.

Bill pointed to the dead man. "Who is he?"

The coroner answered that through lips which were ice blue. "No identification. Even has the clothes marks ripped out of his coat."

"I suppose Joe did that," said Bill, his face very straight.

The coroner made a rough sound in his throat. "This isn't any time for joking, Lacy. I'm about scared out of my skin waiting for that brute to show up."

"You needn't be," replied O'Connor. "He'll be dead before he gets back here."

The coroner looked over his shoulder and the gesture caused Hartman to look over his.

"I think I'll go back to town," said Hartman. "There ain't no use staying around here. That thing . . ."

"It's your gorilla, isn't it?" snapped O'Connor.

Hartman closed his thin mouth and looked about him nervously.

"I think," said Bill Lacy, "that I'll look over the corpse. Any objections?"

"No," said the coroner. "We've finished with it."

"Any fingerprints?" asked Bill.

The fingerprint expert snorted. "Who in hell expects a gorilla to have fingerprints!"

"It isn't a gorilla," replied Bill. "It's an orangutan."

"What's the difference?" snapped the coroner. "If you want to look over the stiff, go ahead."

Bill dragged himself across the intervening ten feet and sat down in the snow beside the blue dead man. Hartman watched him narrowly.

"I think I'll go," said Hartman. "I'm getting cold as hell."

"Stick around," remarked Bill. "The cops will have Joe in no time at all." And then he bent over the dead man and turned the head.

Bill Lacy's cold fingers worked at the coat and finally opened it up. He reached inside and found the label over the inner breast pocket torn out. From there he went on through the garment with careful thoroughness. But he found nothing.

"Where's his hat?" asked Bill.

The coroner tossed him the article in question. "What's eating you, Lacy?"

Bill said nothing. His entire concentration was given to the sweatband. His chilled fingers went around under it and turned it inside out. He placed his flashlight close against it and then grunted.

"Find anything?" asked O'Connor.

For answer the newspaperman held up the sweatband, but he did not offer to release it. "Initials in here," he said. "G. H. G. Mean anything to you?"

"No," said O'Connor. "Where are they?"

"G. H. G. means George Henry Greyson," continued Bill. "This corpse here is Greyson."

Men stopped flailing their arms and looked down at him. Several of them tried to see the sweatband but could not.

Hartman came closer, his mouth open in astonishment. "So! That's the answer to the riddle. Greyson stole that orangutan for some reason. Maybe he had something up his sleeve."

Bill put the band back in place. "Probably so. Probably Greyson knew what Joe was worth in advertising and he intended to steal him. Joe's worth a couple thousand, you know."

Hartman whistled. "That's it. Our trademark, 'Stronger than a gorilla' was eating away into Greyson's own business. Besides, Greyson has had us under his thumb for some little time. He figured that he could humiliate us this way by exhibiting our own ape."

"Sure," said Bill, intent on his thoughts. "Greyson must have brought a couple thugs with him, and when Joe got mad in the car, he broke Greyson's neck and the thugs threw them both out for fear they'd be named as felons or accomplices or something. That sort of lets Joe out, doesn't it?"

"The hell it does," snapped O'Connor. "This gorilla is a killer. He'll have to take the consequences."

And then Bill Lacy said something which was very unexpected. "Where's your evidence that names Joe as the killer?"

O'Connor started to bellow something, but stopped and gave Bill an exasperated stare.

And Bill went on. "Greyson had Hartman and Para Rubber under his thumb. Greyson didn't have to resort to ape stealing."

Hartman glared. "What do you mean? Greyson didn't have anybody under his thumb. He was a two-for-a-cent crook! That's what Greyson was."

Bill grinned slowly. "You didn't like him, did you?"

"Of course not," replied Hartman.

"And you killed him."

Bill's words struck silence to the crowd. All eyes traveled from Bill to the face of the Para president.

"You're crazy," said Hartman, slowly.

"Not so crazy," replied Bill. "Why didn't you identify Greyson for the cops when you first came?"

"Why—why—" Hartman gasped.

"Why did you rip out Greyson's identification after you strangled him? Did you figure he'd be marked as missing and that's all? They've got morgues, Hartman, and morgues are meant for identification. As soon as Greyson disappeared, he'd be looked for in the morgue."

Hartman laughed nervously. "You're seeing things, Lacy."

"Am I?" replied Bill. "There's a couple things you don't know about an orangutan, Hartman."

The crowd was nervous enough already. Hartman's laugh died. The darkness was thick beyond the lights of the crowd which, by contrast, dimmed all men's eyes.

"Yes," said Bill, "there's a couple things you don't know. The orangutan has a marvelous memory. There have been cases where orangutans have suddenly gone mad, plowing through everything to get at anyone who has hurt them."

"Yaw," said O'Connor. "Quit it. You been sayin' . . ."

"Yes, I know," said Bill. "But I didn't know that Hartman

here had cut Joe up before he set him loose. That means that Joe is probably in a blind, red rage. Such a brute would not stop at anything to get at Hartman, to tear his flesh from his bones and snap his neck like it was a match and throw the mangled corpse . . ."

"Quit it!" said Hartman.

"No," said Bill, "you don't know orangutans. There was one case where a hunter shot one and before he could fire again, the orangutan charged straight in and gouged out the hunter's eyes like they were marbles and then ripped out his throat with long, white fangs. . . ."

Nobody spoke as Bill went on. Men were nervous enough already. Eyes raked the darkness beyond them which they could not penetrate.

And suddenly Bill stopped talking and listened intently. Hartman's eyes were wide and staring. He listened too.

Then Bill looked scared. He stepped a pace toward the darkness, staring into it. He appeared very nervous. But he knew that his car was across the road behind him.

Nerves were at the snapping point and O'Connor opened his mouth to bawl Bill out for making such a show. But Bill beat him to it.

With a sudden yelp, Bill threw himself backwards, knocking O'Connor down. Bill grabbed O'Connor's revolver and began to stab flame into the night.

"Don't let him get away!" cried Bill, shooting wildly. "There's the brute! Under that tree! He's charging! Kill him!"

Hartman stood it but an instant. The shots snapped his

strength to stand. Guilt was too heavy in his brain and death was too near.

With men falling back upon him in panic, Hartman was almost knocked down and then the panic hit him.

He whirled and saw Bill's car. With a shriek of terror he raced toward it.

Bill abruptly turned and saw where Hartman had gone, that Hartman had done the right thing for Bill and the wrong one for Hartman.

The police saw nothing under the tree at last as their sweeping flashlights showed.

"What the hell . . . ?" began O'Connor, glaring at Bill.

"Look!" said Bill. "But don't shoot!"

The crowd turned and looked at the coupe. An awful thing had happened.

A pair of great hairy arms shot out and caught Hartman in their embrace. Hartman screamed and the arms tightened.

"The ape!" shrieked O'Connor. "The ape's got him!"

Unmindful of the pain in his ankle, Bill dragged himself across the road to the car. He straightened up, catching hold of the door window for support. But he made no move to drag away Joe's arms or to touch Hartman. Bill was standing there as a shield. No one would shoot at the ape, now.

Hartman was moaning deep in his tortured throat. O'Connor, the newshawks and the police were coming up now, heartened by the sight of Bill's supposed bravery.

"Let me at him!" shouted O'Connor. "I'll drill him."

"Shut up," said Bill, not moving an inch. "The minute you

promise to take Hartman away and Hartman only, I'll let you pass."

"But he'll kill him!" wailed an officer.

"What if he does?" snapped Bill. "Hartman had it coming."

Joe was looking intently over Hartman's quivering shoulders, and his brown eyes saw nothing but Bill. Slowly his arms relaxed and Hartman was allowed to slither out and into the snow. Slowly, Bill closed the coupe door and pointed down.

"Take him," said Bill. "Lock him up. He'll have to stand trial for the murder of Greyson."

"But he's dead," shouted O'Connor, looking at Hartman.

"No, he isn't dead," replied Bill. "Joe was just squeezing him a little, that's all."

And as though in confirmation to Bill's words, Hartman raised himself up and looked at the guns about him. He let his head slump again.

"Don't let him get me," moaned Hartman.

"I will if you don't come clean," snapped Bill, heady with a sudden inspiration. "What happened?"

"I'll tell, only don't let that ape get me!" He looked up with terror-shot eyes at the coupe. He saw Bill's hand fumble with the handle of the door. "Greyson had me," cried Hartman. "He was going to wreck me and he knew I'd taken some money which wasn't mine. He was putting down the screws on me. So I killed him. I choked him to death. And then I put that ape in the car and brought the body out here. When I dumped them, the ape turned on me."

"Why?" said Bill, rattling the handle.

Hartman could see Joe through the glass and he shivered.

"Because I put soap in his mouth and cut his lips so they'd bleed. And then I whipped him so he'd get mad."

Bill Lacy nodded. "Take him away, O'Connor. Better handcuff him, too. He's slippery."

O'Connor knelt and executed the rite. "You're telling me?"

The fingerprint expert shook his head dazedly. "Funny there weren't any fingerprints on Greyson. Hartman must have used gloves."

"Sure he did," said Bill. "If there had been fingerprints, Joe would have been guilty."

"What do you mean?" said the expert.

For answer Bill opened the door and took Joe's long hand. He pulled it toward him gently and turned the light on the fingertips.

"See," said Bill. "There are all the whorls and arches and loops and composites you ever want to see. Apes have fingerprints just like everybody else."

"I'll be doggoned," breathed the expert. "You're right."

"Of course I'm right. That's what made me suspect that Hartman wasn't aboveboard with this thing."

"Funny we missed the initials on that hatband," said the coroner.

Bill grinned and shifted his game foot. "You didn't miss them because they aren't there. I just took a shot in the dark about it, and when Hartman ran, that sealed it for me. Joe wouldn't kill anybody. A little girl down in Oleleh, Sumatra, raised him on a bottle. Well, if you boys have got your prisoner and everything is all right, I guess I'd better be getting to a hospital."

O'Connor nodded and saw for the first time that Bill was hurt. "Can you manage all right?"

"Sure," said Bill. "I'll have to get Joe fixed up, too. He's had a pretty hard night of it and if he don't get attention, he might catch cold."

Bill Lacy climbed into his coupe and motioned for Joe to move over in the seat. When Joe was curled up beside him, Bill started the engine, warmed it and let in the clutch. They slid away from the headlights and the police.

"Well, Joe," said Bill Lacy. "I don't guess you've got any home, now, and though I don't know what in the devil I'm going to do with you, I guess we'll have to be pardners."

Joe assumed an expression which was very much like a smile and decided that it was time for all good orangutans to go to sleep.

Story Preview

Story Preview

NOW that you've just ventured through some of the captivating tales in the Stories from the Golden Age collection by L. Ron Hubbard, turn the page and enjoy a preview of *The Chee-Chalker*. Join FBI Agent Bill Norton in Ketchikan, Alaska, where he discovers an heiress to a bankrupt fishing fleet, a missing G-man and a string of corpses dismissed as "accidental drownings" . . . all leading him to a murderous heroin smuggling ring.

The Chee-Chalker

P AUL WAGNER owned the Tamgas Trading Company
and was a very important man in Ketchikan, even in
Alaska. "Aren't you with the FBI?"

Norton looked at him from under his hat brim.

"Fagler said you were and I wanted to know what you
thought about it. I'm Paul Wagner."

"Well?"

"I wanted to know what you thought about this. It is
serious. James England was an important fellow to Alaska.
His station up there on the knoll is Alaska's biggest and best.
Now what's going to happen to it? I depend on him, or rather
did, for my advertising. What do you make of it?"

"Make of what?" said Norton.

"Why, his murder."

"I thought they said it was suicide."

"They said it was accidental."

"I wasn't listening very closely."

"What do you make of it?"

"Why should I make anything of it? It's none of my
business."

"I thought you were in town to look into his disappearance."

"Did you?"

"Well," said Wagner, his dark face turned full on Norton

now, "that was my impression. The Federal marshal wasn't making any progress and so I thought you had been sent down to look into it."

"Know anything about it?"

"About his disappearance?"

"Yes."

Wagner looked closely at Norton but he couldn't see through the rain and shadows well enough. "I know no more than anybody else. He had no enemies in particular and he was well loved."

"I heard differently," said Norton.

"No man is worth his salt who hasn't a few enemies," said Wagner nervously. He stayed around for nearly a minute but nothing more was said and so, uncomfortably, he went away.

Norton was glad he had gone. He wanted some more cold rain on his face. He wished corpses weren't a part of a lawman's business. At times like these he intensely regretted the small gold disc pinned to his wallet. That small gold disc sent him to such unseemly places.

Ketchikan, for example.

He looked at the rain and wondered that the skies were never emptied. A hundred and eighty inches a year was a tropical output with none of the tropical advantages. Of course it wasn't as cold here as it was in Juneau. Far north though it was, it was as warm through the winter as most of the US coastal towns. If only it wouldn't rain.

Bill Norton did not much like this country. He had been in it six months, most of the six spent behind a desk in Juneau, the last spent wandering around Ketchikan trying to get a lead on a sack of "snow" and Jerry McCain. He had found the heroin leading nowhere so far as he could discover. And he had found no sign of FBI special agent Jerry McCain. There was no more "snow." There was no trail whatever leading to the disappearance of his former boss. There was only rain. Rain and bars and drunken Indians and soldiers much drunker. Bill Norton, looking at the bobbing masthead and boom of a halibut boat tied to the Tamgas dock, was reminded of a gibbet.

Up the slippery boards skated a burblingly active young man, one of Bill's main responsibilities. Chick Star had just graduated from the School in Washington. Some clerk had sent him to Alaska on the first boat. Chick wore people out.

"What's the excitement?" said Chick.

"Corpse," said Norton diffidently.

"Aw, honest? Who, where?"

"England. Drowned."

"Gee! You finally located England? Gosh! Say, that's good work! Gosh, why wasn't I around?"

"If you'd stop chasing klootches you might get in on something sometime," said Norton, bored.

"Klootches," said Chick in a hurt voice. "I don't chase klootches. I can't stand the sight of an Indian. Why would I chase klootches?"

He was so earnestly involved, so gashed to the marrow, that Norton looked at him. Chick was six feet seven. He weighed two hundred and eighteen pounds. He ran into and knocked over things. He was twenty-three and serious. He was full of ambition. He polished his gold disc every night before he went to bed and carried his heavy Colt revolver to dances.

"If you don't you'll go nutty with this rain," said Norton.

"Oh, I like the rain," said Chick. "It's exciting. Things are dark and mysterious. Where'd you find England?"

"I didn't find him."

"But you must have," said Chick, gloatingly surveying his hero. "Was he stabbed?"

"He fell in and hit his head on a piling. The fish ate his face."

"Aw."

"Well if you can't take it you've got no business hanging around the Bureau."

"You're being modest," said Chick hopefully. "You found him and he was murdered and you know who did it."

"Sherlock Holmes doesn't happen to be even a faint relation of mine," said Norton. He slogged through the horizontal sea in the air toward bed at the Sourdough Hotel.

"Say!" said Chick, "did you see that?"

"What?"

"Those two men come out from behind that truck and turn the corner up there. They looked suspicious!"

"If they're suspicious you've given them plenty of warning with that brass voice of yours."

"Honest they did."

"Probably were having a quiet drink where their pals wouldn't ask for any."

Chick loped up beside Norton, splashing heavily through the puddles like an overgrown tank and thoroughly spattering his despondent boss. Suddenly Chick threw out his arm to stop Norton and almost knocked him flat backwards on the slippery boardwalk.

"Look at that!" said Chick in what he hopefully supposed to be a whisper.

A young woman had come out of the door of the Sourdough Hotel ahead of them. The lights from the windows were not sufficient to show her features but they were ample to bring into silhouette the two men who emerged from an alleyway. The silhouettes swooped down upon the young woman and grabbed her. Hurriedly they led her straight toward the dock. They evidently did not see Chick and Norton standing on the walk before them for all was blackness in that direction.

"Take your hands off me!" protested a girl's voice.

"Come along," said one of her captors.

Norton was always faintly nervous when he was with Chick. He could never be sure what Chick would do. Chick would follow orders after a fashion—with a few "improvements" of his own—but when Chick had no specific orders, anything might happen.

To find out more about *The Chee-Chalker* and how you can obtain your copy, go to www.goldenagestories.com.

Glossary

STORIES FROM THE GOLDEN AGE *reflect the words and expressions used in the 1930s and 1940s, adding unique flavor and authenticity to the tales. While a character's speech may often reflect regional origins, it also can convey attitudes common in the day. So that readers can better grasp such cultural and historical terms, uncommon words or expressions of the era, the following glossary has been provided.*

"begorrah": (Irish) used as an exclamation or a mild oath; alteration of "by God."

binnacle: a built-in housing for a ship's compass.

bitt: a vertical post, usually one of a pair, set on the deck of a ship and used for securing cables, lines for towing, etc.

Black Maria: patrol wagon; an enclosed truck or van used by the police to transport prisoners.

bowler: derby; a hard felt hat with a rounded crown and narrow brim, created by James Lock & Co, a firm founded in 1676 in London. The prototype was made in 1850 for a customer of Lock's by Thomas and William Bowler, hat makers in Southwark, England. At first it was dubbed the *iron hat* because it was hard enough to protect the head, and later picked up the name *bowler* because of its makers' family name. In the US it became known as a *derby* from its association with the Kentucky Derby.

bows: the exterior of the forward end of a vessel.

bracelets: a pair of handcuffs.

buck up: take courage; take heart.

bump: to kill.

chee-chalker: a newcomer to Alaska and the Klondike; an Indian word meaning one who is inexperienced or has no knowledge; a tenderfoot.

Colt revolver: Colt Detective Special; a short-barreled revolver first produced in 1927 by the Colt Firearms Company. Though originally offered as a .32 caliber, the most common of the Colt Detective Specials were .38 caliber and had a two-inch barrel. The short barrel design made this gun popular for use as a concealed weapon by plainclothes police detectives.

coyote: used for a man who has the sneaking and skulking characteristics of a coyote.

cuspidor: a large bowl, often of metal, serving as a receptacle for spit, especially from chewing tobacco, in wide use during the nineteenth and early twentieth centuries.

cutter: 1. a ship's boat, powered by a motor or oars and used for transporting stores or passengers. 2. a type of US Coast Guard vessel that is over 65 feet in length. *Cutter* originally referred to a small, single-masted vessel, fore-and-aft rigged with two or more headsails. The term was adopted by the US Treasury Department when the US Revenue Cutter

Service was formed in 1790, which then became the US Coast Guard in 1915, and *cutter* has come to mean a small armed vessel in government service.

davit: a cranelike device, used singly or in pairs, for supporting, raising and lowering boats, anchors and cargo over a hatchway or side of a ship.

dick: a detective.

drill: shoot.

durian: a tree native to the tropical rain forests of Southeast Asia that bears a foul-smelling but deliciously flavored fruit. The seeds are roasted and eaten like nuts.

El: elevated railway.

fo'c's'le: forecastle; the upper deck of a sailing ship, forward of the foremast.

forty-five or **.45 automatic:** a handgun chambered to fire a .45-caliber cartridge and that utilizes the recoil or part of the force of the explosive to eject the spent cartridge shell, introduce a new cartridge, cock the arm and fire it repeatedly.

gibbet: an upright post with a crosspiece, forming a T-shaped structure from which criminals were formerly hanged for public viewing.

G-men: government men; agents of the Federal Bureau of Investigation.

greenhorn: an easterner unacquainted with cowboy ways.

gum: interfere with.

Havana: a seaport in and the capital of Cuba, on the northwest coast.

hawser: a thick rope or cable for mooring or towing a ship.

hempen: made of hemp, the fiber from the hemp plant used to make canvas, rope, etc.

horned spoon, by the great: a "horned spoon" is a tool made from a cow horn. The saying "by the great horned spoon" was at one time a fairly common American oath and used to make a statement emphatic. Its first recorded usage was in 1842.

jaspers: fellows; guys.

Judge Colt: nickname for the single-action (that is, cocked by hand for each shot), six-shot Army model revolver first produced in 1873 by Colt Firearms Company, the armory founded by Samuel Colt (1814–1862). The handgun of the Old West became the instrument of both lawmaker and lawbreaker during the last twenty-five years of the nineteenth century. It soon earned various names, such as "Peacemaker," "Equalizer," and "Judge Colt and his jury of six."

Juneau: port city in southeastern Alaska. In 1900 it was made the capital of the territory of Alaska and later the state capital when Alaska joined the Union in 1959. It is named after the gold prospector Joseph Juneau, who discovered gold in the area in 1880.

kapok: a silky fiber obtained from the fruit of the silk-cotton tree and used for insulation and as padding in pillows, mattresses and life preservers.

Ketchikan: a city located on the southwestern coast of Revillagigedo Island near the southern boundary of Alaska, and named after the Ketchikan Creek that flows through the town. Much of the town sits over water, supported by pilings. Ketchikan has the heaviest average rainfall in North America and is one of the four wettest spots on Earth. With 160 inches of rain a year, the rainfall is measured in feet, not inches. The locals refer to rain as "liquid sunshine."

klootches: Indian women of northwestern Alaska.

lobo: wolf; one who is regarded as predatory, greedy and fierce.

material witness: a witness whose testimony is both relevant to the matter at issue and required in order to resolve the matter.

monkey fist: a ball-like knot used as an ornament or as a throwing weight at the end of a line.

newshawk: a newspaper reporter, especially one who is energetic and aggressive.

Oleleh: Oleleh Harbor; a harbor on the Island of Sumatra.

pannin': panning; criticizing or reviewing harshly; giving an unfavorable review of.

paper suitcase: an inexpensive suitcase made of hard cardboard.

Police Positive .38: Colt Police Positive; a .38-caliber revolver developed by the Colt Firearms Company in answer to a demand for a more powerful version of the .32-caliber Police Positive. First introduced in 1905, these guns were sold to many US police forces and European military units, as well as being made available to the general public.

Punch: the chief male character of the Punch and Judy puppet show, a famous English comedy dating back to the seventeenth century, by way of France from Italy. It is performed using hand puppets in a tent-style puppet theater with a cloth backdrop and board in front. The puppeteer introduces the puppets from beneath the board so that they are essentially popping up to the stage area of the theater.

rod: another name for a handgun.

roscoe: another name for a handgun.

rowels: the small spiked revolving wheels on the ends of spurs, which are attached to the heels of a rider's boots and used to nudge a horse into going faster.

rubber hose: a piece of hose made of rubber, used to beat people as a form of torture or in order to obtain a full or partial confession and to elicit information. A rubber hose was used because its blows, while painful, leave only slight marks on the body of the person beaten.

sap: dumb guy; a fool.

Scheherazade: the female narrator of *The Arabian Nights,* who during one thousand and one adventurous nights saved her life by entertaining her husband, the king, with stories.

shivved: knifed; stabbed with a shiv (knife).

shorthorn: a tenderfoot; a newcomer or a person not used to rough living and hardships.

sidewinder: rattlesnake.

slick-ear: "wet behind the ears"; someone who is inexperienced or naïve.

slickers: swindlers; sly cheats.

slug: a bullet.

"snow": cocaine or heroin in the form of a white powder.

SOS: the letters represented by the radio telegraphic signal known as Morse code, used especially by ships in distress, as an internationally recognized call for help.

spittoon: a container for spitting into.

SS: steamship.

stateroom: a private room or compartment on a train, ship, etc.

stay: any of various strong ropes or wires for steadying masts.

stern: the rear end of a ship or boat.

Sumatra: a large island in the western part of Indonesia. Most of Sumatra used to be covered by tropical rainforest.

'tween decks: between decks; spaces between two continuous decks in the hull of a vessel.

two bits: a quarter; during the colonial days, people used coins from all over the world. When the US adopted an official currency, the Spanish milled (machine-struck) dollar was chosen and it later became the model for American silver dollars. Milled dollars were easily cut apart into equal "bits" of eight pieces. Two bits would equal a quarter of a dollar.

well deck: the space on the main deck of a ship lying at a lower level between the bridge and either a raised forward deck or a raised deck at the stern, which usually has cabins underneath.

West Indies: a group of islands in the North Atlantic between North and South America, comprising the Greater Antilles, the Lesser Antilles and the Bahamas.

wisenheimer: smart aleck; wise guy; one who is obnoxiously self-assertive and arrogant.

L. Ron Hubbard
in the Golden Age
of Pulp Fiction

*In writing an adventure story
a writer has to know that he is adventuring
for a lot of people who cannot.
The writer has to take them here and there
about the globe and show them
excitement and love and realism.
As long as that writer is living the part of an
adventurer when he is hammering
the keys, he is succeeding with his story.*

*Adventuring is a state of mind.
If you adventure through life, you have a
good chance to be a success on paper.*

*Adventure doesn't mean globe-trotting,
exactly, and it doesn't mean great deeds.
Adventuring is like art.
You have to live it to make it real.*

—*L. RON HUBBARD*

L. Ron Hubbard
and American
Pulp Fiction

B ORN March 13, 1911, L. Ron Hubbard lived a life at least as expansive as the stories with which he enthralled a hundred million readers through a fifty-year career.

Originally hailing from Tilden, Nebraska, he spent his formative years in a classically rugged Montana, replete with the cowpunchers, lawmen and desperadoes who would later people his Wild West adventures. And lest anyone imagine those adventures were drawn from vicarious experience, he was not only breaking broncs at a tender age, he was also among the few whites ever admitted into Blackfoot society as a bona fide blood brother. While if only to round out an otherwise rough and tumble youth, his mother was that rarity of her time—a thoroughly educated woman—who introduced her son to the classics of Occidental literature even before his seventh birthday.

But as any dedicated L. Ron Hubbard reader will attest, his world extended far beyond Montana. In point of fact, and as the son of a United States naval officer, by the age of eighteen he had traveled over a quarter of a million miles. Included therein were three Pacific crossings to a then still mysterious Asia, where he ran with the likes of Her British Majesty's agent-in-place

L. Ron Hubbard, left, at Congressional Airport, Washington, DC, 1931, with members of George Washington University flying club.

for North China, and the last in the line of Royal Magicians from the court of Kublai Khan. For the record, L. Ron Hubbard was also among the first Westerners to gain admittance to forbidden Tibetan monasteries below Manchuria, and his photographs of China's Great Wall long graced American geography texts.

Upon his return to the United States and a hasty completion of his interrupted high school education, the young Ron Hubbard entered George Washington University. There, as fans of his aerial adventures may have heard, he earned his wings as a pioneering barnstormer at the dawn of American aviation. He also earned a place in free-flight record books for the longest sustained flight above Chicago. Moreover, as a roving reporter for *Sportsman Pilot* (featuring his first professionally penned articles), he further helped inspire a generation of pilots who would take America to world airpower.

Immediately beyond his sophomore year, Ron embarked on the first of his famed ethnological expeditions, initially to then untrammeled Caribbean shores (descriptions of which would later fill a whole series of West Indies mystery-thrillers). That the Puerto Rican interior would also figure into the future of Ron Hubbard stories was likewise no accident. For in addition to cultural studies of the island, a 1932–33

LRH expedition is rightly remembered as conducting the first complete mineralogical survey of a Puerto Rico under United States jurisdiction.

There was many another adventure along this vein: As a lifetime member of the famed Explorers Club, L. Ron Hubbard charted North Pacific waters with the first shipboard radio direction finder, and so pioneered a long-range navigation system universally employed until the late twentieth century. While not to put too fine an edge on it, he also held a rare Master Mariner's license to pilot any vessel, of any tonnage in any ocean.

Yet lest we stray too far afield, there is an LRH note at this juncture in his saga, and it reads in part:

"I started out writing for the pulps, writing the best I knew, writing for every mag on the stands, slanting as well as I could."

Capt. L. Ron Hubbard in Ketchikan, Alaska, 1940, on his Alaskan Radio Experimental Expedition, the first of three voyages conducted under the Explorers Club flag.

To which one might add: His earliest submissions date from the summer of 1934, and included tales drawn from true-to-life Asian adventures, with characters roughly modeled on British/American intelligence operatives he had known in Shanghai. His early Westerns were similarly peppered with details drawn from personal experience. Although therein lay a first hard lesson from the often cruel world of the pulps. His first Westerns were soundly rejected as lacking the authenticity of a Max Brand yarn (a particularly frustrating comment given L. Ron Hubbard's Westerns came straight from his Montana homeland, while Max Brand was a mediocre New York poet named Frederick Schiller Faust, who turned out implausible six-shooter tales from the terrace of an Italian villa).

Nevertheless, and needless to say, L. Ron Hubbard persevered and soon earned a reputation as among the most publishable names in pulp fiction, with a ninety percent placement rate of first-draft manuscripts. He was also among the most prolific, averaging between seventy and a hundred thousand words a month. Hence the rumors that L. Ron Hubbard had redesigned a typewriter for faster keyboard action and pounded out manuscripts on a continuous roll of butcher paper to save the precious seconds it took to insert a single sheet of paper into manual typewriters of the day.

That all L. Ron Hubbard stories did not run beneath said byline is yet another aspect of pulp fiction lore. That is, as publishers periodically rejected manuscripts from top-drawer authors if only to avoid paying top dollar, L. Ron Hubbard and company just as frequently replied with submissions under various pseudonyms. In Ron's case, the list

A MAN OF MANY NAMES

Between 1934 and 1950, L. Ron Hubbard authored more than fifteen million words of fiction in more than two hundred classic publications. To supply his fans and editors with stories across an array of genres and pulp titles, he adopted fifteen pseudonyms in addition to his already renowned L. Ron Hubbard byline.

Winchester Remington Colt
Lt. Jonathan Daly
Capt. Charles Gordon
Capt. L. Ron Hubbard
Bernard Hubbel
Michael Keith
Rene Lafayette
Legionnaire 148
Legionnaire 14830
Ken Martin
Scott Morgan
Lt. Scott Morgan
Kurt von Rachen
Barry Randolph
Capt. Humbert Reynolds

included: Rene Lafayette, Captain Charles Gordon, Lt. Scott Morgan and the notorious Kurt von Rachen—supposedly on the lam for a murder rap, while hammering out two-fisted prose in Argentina. The point: While L. Ron Hubbard as Ken Martin spun stories of Southeast Asian intrigue, LRH as Barry Randolph authored tales of romance on the Western range—which, stretching between a dozen genres is how he came to stand among the two hundred elite authors providing close to a million tales through the glory days of American Pulp Fiction.

L. Ron Hubbard, circa 1930, at the outset of a literary career that would finally span half a century.

In evidence of exactly that, by 1936 L. Ron Hubbard was literally leading pulp fiction's elite as president of New York's American Fiction Guild. Members included a veritable pulp hall of fame: Lester "Doc Savage" Dent, Walter "The Shadow" Gibson, and the legendary Dashiell Hammett—to cite but a few.

Also in evidence of just where L. Ron Hubbard stood within his first two years on the American pulp circuit: By the spring of 1937, he was ensconced in Hollywood, adopting a Caribbean thriller for Columbia Pictures, remembered today as *The Secret of Treasure Island.* Comprising fifteen thirty-minute episodes, the L. Ron Hubbard screenplay led to the most profitable matinée serial in Hollywood history. In accord with Hollywood culture, he was thereafter continually called

The 1937 Secret of Treasure Island, *a fifteen-episode serial adapted for the screen by L. Ron Hubbard from his novel,* Murder at Pirate Castle.

upon to rewrite/doctor scripts—most famously for long-time friend and fellow adventurer Clark Gable.

In the interim—and herein lies another distinctive chapter of the L. Ron Hubbard story—he continually worked to open Pulp Kingdom gates to up-and-coming authors. Or, for that matter, anyone who wished to write. It was a fairly unconventional stance, as markets were already thin and competition razor sharp. But the fact remains, it was an L. Ron Hubbard hallmark that he vehemently lobbied on behalf of young authors—regularly supplying instructional articles to trade journals, guest-lecturing to short story classes at George Washington University and Harvard, and even founding his own creative writing competition. It was established in 1940, dubbed the Golden Pen, and guaranteed winners both New York representation and publication in *Argosy*.

But it was John W. Campbell Jr.'s *Astounding Science Fiction* that finally proved the most memorable LRH vehicle. While every fan of L. Ron Hubbard's galactic epics undoubtedly knows the story, it nonetheless bears repeating: By late 1938, the pulp publishing magnate of Street & Smith was determined to revamp *Astounding Science Fiction* for broader readership. In particular, senior editorial director F. Orlin Tremaine called for stories with a stronger *human element*. When acting editor John W. Campbell balked, preferring his spaceship-driven tales,

Tremaine enlisted Hubbard. Hubbard, in turn, replied with the genre's first truly *character-driven* works, wherein heroes are pitted not against bug-eyed monsters but the mystery and majesty of deep space itself—and thus was launched the Golden Age of Science Fiction.

The names alone are enough to quicken the pulse of any science fiction aficionado, including LRH friend and protégé, Robert Heinlein, Isaac Asimov, A. E. van Vogt and Ray Bradbury. Moreover, when coupled with LRH stories of fantasy, we further come to what's rightly been described as the foundation of every modern tale of horror: L. Ron Hubbard's immortal *Fear*. It was rightly proclaimed by Stephen King as one of the very few works to genuinely warrant that overworked term "classic"—as in: *"This is a classic tale of creeping, surreal menace and horror. . . . This is one of the really, really good ones."*

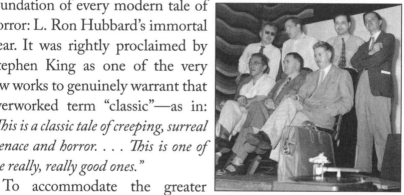

L. Ron Hubbard, 1948, among fellow science fiction luminaries at the World Science Fiction Convention in Toronto.

To accommodate the greater body of L. Ron Hubbard fantasies, Street & Smith inaugurated *Unknown*—a classic pulp if there ever was one, and wherein readers were soon thrilling to the likes of *Typewriter in the Sky* and *Slaves of Sleep* of which Frederik Pohl would declare: *"There are bits and pieces from Ron's work that became part of the language in ways that very few other writers managed."*

And, indeed, at J. W. Campbell Jr.'s insistence, Ron was regularly drawing on themes from the Arabian Nights and so introducing readers to a world of genies, jinn, Aladdin and Sinbad—all of which, of course, continue to float through cultural mythology to this day.

At least as influential in terms of post-apocalypse stories was L. Ron Hubbard's 1940 *Final Blackout*. Generally acclaimed as the finest anti-war novel of the decade and among the ten best works of the genre ever authored—here, too, was a tale that would live on in ways few other writers

imagined. Hence, the later Robert Heinlein verdict: "Final Blackout *is as perfect a piece of science fiction as has ever been written.*"

Like many another who both lived and wrote American pulp adventure, the war proved a tragic end to Ron's sojourn in the pulps. He served with distinction in four theaters and was highly decorated for commanding corvettes in the North Pacific. He was also grievously wounded in combat, lost many a close friend and colleague and thus resolved to say farewell to pulp fiction and devote himself to what it had supported these many years—namely, his serious research.

Portland, Oregon, 1943; L. Ron Hubbard captain of the US Navy subchaser PC 815.

But in no way was the LRH literary saga at an end, for as he wrote some thirty years later, in 1980:

"Recently there came a period when I had little to do. This was novel in a life so crammed with busy years, and I decided to amuse myself by writing a novel that was pure science fiction."

That work was *Battlefield Earth: A Saga of the Year 3000*. It was an immediate *New York Times* bestseller and, in fact, the first international science fiction blockbuster in decades. It was not, however, L. Ron Hubbard's magnum opus, as that distinction is generally reserved for his next and final work: The 1.2 million word *Mission Earth*.

> **Final Blackout**
> *is as perfect a piece of science fiction as has ever been written.*
>
> —Robert Heinlein

How he managed those 1.2 million words in just over twelve months is yet another piece of the L. Ron Hubbard legend. But the fact remains, he did indeed author a ten-volume *dekalogy* that lives in publishing history for the fact that each and every volume of the series was also a *New York Times* bestseller.

Moreover, as subsequent generations discovered L. Ron Hubbard through republished works and novelizations of his screenplays, the mere fact of his name on a cover signaled an international bestseller. . . . Until, to date, sales of his works exceed hundreds of millions, and he otherwise remains among the most enduring and widely read authors in literary history. Although as a final word on the tales of L. Ron Hubbard, perhaps it's enough to simply reiterate what editors told readers in the glory days of American Pulp Fiction:

He writes the way he does, brothers, because he's been there, seen it and done it!

THE STORIES FROM THE
GOLDEN AGE

Your ticket to adventure starts here with the Stories from
the Golden Age collection by master storyteller L. Ron Hubbard.
These gripping tales are set in a kaleidoscope of exotic locales and brim
with fascinating characters, including some of the
most vile villains, dangerous dames and brazen heroes
you'll ever get to meet.

The entire collection of over one hundred and fifty stories is being
released in a series of eighty books and audiobooks.
For an up-to-date listing of available titles,
go to www.goldenagestories.com.

AIR ADVENTURE

Arctic Wings
The Battling Pilot
Boomerang Bomber
The Crate Killer
The Dive Bomber
Forbidden Gold
Hurtling Wings
The Lieutenant Takes the Sky

Man-Killers of the Air
On Blazing Wings
Red Death Over China
Sabotage in the Sky
Sky Birds Dare!
The Sky-Crasher
Trouble on His Wings
Wings Over Ethiopia

FAR-FLUNG ADVENTURE

The Adventure of "X"
All Frontiers Are Jealous
The Barbarians
The Black Sultan
Black Towers to Danger
The Bold Dare All
Buckley Plays a Hunch
The Cossack
Destiny's Drum
Escape for Three
Fifty-Fifty O'Brien
The Headhunters
Hell's Legionnaire
He Walked to War
Hostage to Death

Hurricane
The Iron Duke
Machine Gun 21,000
Medals for Mahoney
Price of a Hat
Red Sand
The Sky Devil
The Small Boss of Nunaloha
The Squad That Never Came Back
Starch and Stripes
Tomb of the Ten Thousand Dead
Trick Soldier
While Bugles Blow!
Yukon Madness

SEA ADVENTURE

Cargo of Coffins
The Drowned City
False Cargo
Grounded
Loot of the Shanung
Mister Tidwell, Gunner

The Phantom Patrol
Sea Fangs
Submarine
Twenty Fathoms Down
Under the Black Ensign

TALES FROM THE ORIENT

The Devil—With Wings *Pearl Pirate*
The Falcon Killer *The Red Dragon*
Five Mex for a Million *Spy Killer*
Golden Hell *Tah*
The Green God *The Trail of the Red Diamonds*
Hurricane's Roar *Wind-Gone-Mad*
Inky Odds *Yellow Loot*
Orders Is Orders

MYSTERY

The Blow Torch Murder *The Grease Spot*
Brass Keys to Murder *Killer Ape*
Calling Squad Cars! *Killer's Law*
The Carnival of Death *The Mad Dog Murder*
The Chee-Chalker *Mouthpiece*
Dead Men Kill *Murder Afloat*
The Death Flyer *The Slickers*
Flame City *They Killed Him Dead*

FANTASY

Borrowed Glory   If I Were You
The Crossroads   The Last Drop
Danger in the Dark   The Room
The Devil's Rescue   The Tramp
He Didn't Like Cats

SCIENCE FICTION

The Automagic Horse   A Matter of Matter
Battle of Wizards   The Obsolete Weapon
Battling Bolto   One Was Stubborn
The Beast   The Planet Makers
Beyond All Weapons   The Professor Was a Thief
A Can of Vacuum   The Slaver
The Conroy Diary   Space Can
The Dangerous Dimension   Strain
Final Enemy   Tough Old Man
The Great Secret   240,000 Miles Straight Up
Greed   When Shadows Fall
The Invaders

WESTERN

The Baron of Coyote River
Blood on His Spurs
Boss of the Lazy B
Branded Outlaw
Cattle King for a Day
Come and Get It
Death Waits at Sundown
Devil's Manhunt
The Ghost Town Gun-Ghost
Gun Boss of Tumbleweed
Gunman!
Gunman's Tally
The Gunner from Gehenna
Hoss Tamer
Johnny, the Town Tamer
King of the Gunmen
The Magic Quirt

Man for Breakfast
The No-Gun Gunhawk
The No-Gun Man
The Ranch That No One Would Buy
Reign of the Gila Monster
Ride 'Em, Cowboy
Ruin at Rio Piedras
Shadows from Boot Hill
Silent Pards
Six-Gun Caballero
Stacked Bullets
Stranger in Town
Tinhorn's Daughter
The Toughest Ranger
Under the Diehard Brand
Vengeance Is Mine!
When Gilhooly Was in Flower

Crash into Ketchikan
to Seize a Killer!

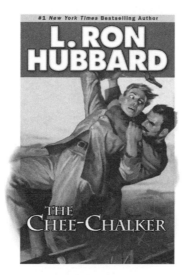

*C*hee-Chalker: *a newcomer or tenderfoot.* Bill Norton might be new to Ketchikan but he's no tenderfoot. In fact, he's an FBI agent—savvy, tough and resourceful, like Harrison Ford as Jack Ryan in *Clear and Present Danger.* Norton's looking for his boss, who vanished investigating a heroin smuggling ring. What Norton finds is murder . . . and a heart-stopping heiress. But is she, too, mixed up in the heroin trade? It will take all of Norton's CSI-like skills to squeeze out the truth.

The action crackles and the romance sizzles as the audio version of *The Chee-Chalker* puts you on the case in a place where the suspense is murder.

Get
The Chee-Chalker

PAPERBACK: **$9.95** OR AUDIOBOOK: **$12.95**
Free Shipping & Handling for Book Club Members
CALL TOLL-FREE: 1-877-8GALAXY (1-877-842-5299)
OR GO ONLINE TO **www.goldenagestories.com**

Galaxy Press, 7051 Hollywood Blvd., Suite 200, Hollywood, CA 90028

JOIN THE PULP REVIVAL
America in the 1930s and 40s

Pulp fiction was in its heyday and 30 million readers were regularly riveted by the larger-than-life tales of master storyteller L. Ron Hubbard. For this was pulp fiction's golden age, when the writing was raw and every page packed a walloping punch.

That magic can now be yours. An evocative world of nefarious villains, exotic intrigues, courageous heroes and heroines—a world that today's cinema has barely tapped for tales of adventure and swashbucklers.

Enroll today in the Stories from the Golden Age Club and begin receiving your monthly feature edition selected from more than 150 stories in the collection.

You may choose to enjoy them as either a paperback or audiobook for the special membership price of $9.95 each month along with FREE shipping and handling.